Lighthouse Inn Mystery #7
The Series Finale

RING FOR MURDER

By

TIM MYERS

D1525535

For Patty, who urged me to begin,
and Emily, who suggested I finally finish.

Chapter 1

In all the years that Hatteras West had stood as a sentinel in the mountains looking down on the Winston clan from birth to death, there had never been such a wondrous occasion to celebrate.

Alex Winston and the love of his life, Elise Danton, were finally getting married.

At least that had been the plan until the dead body appeared.

Chapter 2

"I can't believe we're actually getting married in two days," Elise Danton said to Alex Winston as they watched the sunset together from high atop the Hatteras West lighthouse, their favorite place on earth. The buildings below, a replica of the Main Keeper's Quarters and the Dual Keepers' Quarters that now served as their inn, added to the surreal look of their property, but nothing stood out from the landscape more than their lighthouse. After all, it was located in the foothills of the Blue Ridge Mountains, and not on the North Carolina Outer Banks where its twin stood. Nearby, Bear Rocks shone in the fading light, and the weathered stone seemed to glow as the sun faded away. Alex was tempted to light the beacon just behind them, but it had taken special permission to fire it, and he was saving that for his wedding day.

He squeezed her hand. "It's nearly impossible for me to believe it myself."

"You're not having second thoughts, are you?" Elise asked. "I know you thought you were dying when you proposed to me."

He shook his head. Elise's dark hair caught flashes of the dying sunlight, and her face was framed with a warm glow that Alex wasn't entirely sure was due to the sunset. "That just helped me finally realize what I'd wanted to do for ages. I wanted to propose to you from almost the moment we met."

"Because of the way I looked?" she asked. Alex was well aware of the fact that, though Elise was beautiful, she hated to be judged for her outward appearance alone.

"No, honestly, it was more because of the way you weren't afraid to wax the floors in the lobby."

She smiled at him. "That is exactly the right answer."

Alex had once met Peter Asheford, Elise's first fiancé, a

man who had valued her for her looks and not her substance. He'd lost her, and Alex had found her, to his eternal joy and delight. In all honesty, without Elise by his side over the past few years, he would have never been able to run the inn. She was everything his previous maid, her cousin, Marisa, had not.

"I can't believe Marisa is going to be one of your bridesmaids," Alex said.

She snuggled a little closer to him. "Hey, if she hadn't quit on you and recommended me to take her place, we never would have met."

Alex well remembered the first time Elise had come to Hatteras West. "I'm just glad you didn't run off when we found a dead body."

She shrugged and rubbed his shoulder lightly. "It's all part of an innkeeper's life."

"Murder?" he asked.

"No, thank goodness, not that, but people do get born and die in rooms on occasion, though I'll grant you, we have a tendency toward more murders than births."

Alex was too happy to allow himself to think about the guests they had lost in the past at the inn. It was time to change the subject to something more pleasant. "When are your folks getting into town?"

"All they'd say was that they'd be here in time for the rehearsal dinner tomorrow night."

Alex whistled softly. "That's cutting it close, isn't it?"

"You know better than most folks how tough it is to get away from an inn," she said with a smile. "I've been after them to take some time off, but you know how that goes. They'll be here when it counts." He watched as Elise took a deep breath, and then asked, "Is your brother still coming?"

"I'm not sure," Alex admitted. He and his only sibling Tony were distant at the best of times, and though Alex had invited him to be in the wedding party out of a sense of obligation more than anything else, Tony had declined. He hadn't even been willing to commit to attending the ceremony, and Alex was at least a little relieved that he might not be there at all. He and Tony might have shared a common bloodline, but Mor Pendleton was more of a brother to Alex than Tony had ever been.

"You've still got Mor, don't you?" Elise asked.

"And you've got Emma."

The married couple was serving as their witnesses, best man and matron of honor, and Alex and Elise couldn't have been more pleased about it. Everyone in town they cared about would be there, a celebration to commemorate the love that folks had watched blossom over the years.

Elise shivered a little. "It's getting chilly, isn't it?"

"October can be like that in the foothills," Alex agreed.

"Are you sure you want to get married on your birthday?" she asked him. "It's not too late to change it."

Alex studied her expression for a moment, having a difficult time reading it in the fading light. "You don't have a problem with getting married on Halloween, do you?"

Elise shook her head. "Of course not. I just hope our guests don't show up in costume."

"Some of them are bound to," Alex admitted with a laugh. He touched the lighthouse again, almost as though it were a talisman for him, a way of being certain that all of this was really happening. "I was born right here, and getting married on the steps below is the best way I can think of to celebrate my life so far."

"I agree. If we couldn't get married at the lighthouse, it just wouldn't be the same, would it?"

Alex was thrilled once again that Hatteras West was as much a part of Elise's life as it was his. No matter where he'd traveled in his life, no matter how far he'd been from home, this was where he belonged, and he knew it. His ties to the structures, to the very land beneath his feet, were binding in a way that few folks could ever understand.

He was just glad that Elise was one of the ones who could.

However, she was right. It was getting chilly. "How

about a fire tonight?"

She nodded. "That sounds wonderful."

Twenty minutes later, they were sitting on the floor of the lobby in front of the growing fire. Alex was about to kiss Elise when the front door blew open.

"I made it," Alex's brother, Tony, said, as he stumbled in. Alex couldn't believe it. Was his worthless brother actually drunk?

Alex stood and moved quickly to him. Tony was wearing a black suit, as though he were in mourning; his tie was askew, though the top button of his shirt was still firmly in place, and both his shoes were untied. "Tony, I wasn't sure you were going to make it."

"Can't have my bro get married tomorrow without me," he said.

"It's not tomorrow. It's the day after."

"Whatever," Tony said as he waved a hand in the air, and then looked over at Elise. "How about a good luck kiss from the bride, sweetie?"

Standing close to him, Alex could smell the liquor on his brother's breath. "Why don't we save that for the wedding reception? Maybe you'd like to freshen up a bit. We've got you in the Mountain Laurel Suite."

"What happened to room numbers?" Tony asked as he looked indignantly at his brother. "It was good enough for Mom and Dad. Why isn't it good enough for you? You puttin' on airs, bro?"

Alex and Elise had changed the room numbers to names they felt were more fitting to the inn's surroundings, and though Alex hadn't been sure about it first, he'd grown to love the descriptive names they'd used.

"It used to be room five, if that will make you happy."

"Good ol' number five," Tony said. "Always liked that room."

Elise collected the key and slipped it to Alex, then stepped quickly away before Tony could land claim to the kiss he was clearly expecting.

"Let's go, Tony," Alex said as he helped his brother up the steps. As they climbed, he turned back to Elise and mouthed the words, "Be right back. Sorry."

She nodded with understanding, and Alex focused on getting his brother upstairs and into his bed. "She's a real peach," Tony said as Alex led him down the hallway. "An absolute peach."

"I think so," Alex said as he tried to fit the key in the lock.

The wrought iron sign for the room was fastened above the door, and Tony admired it for a moment. "Sign's kinda nice after all."

"We like it." Alex opened the room door, and nearly let his brother fall in the process. It would serve him right, but Tony was a guest at Hatteras West, and Alex was going to do everything he could to make his brother comfortable, no matter what.

Alex led him to the bed, but Tony refused to cooperate. "We need to talk," he said, slurring his words again, fighting to remain standing.

"I'm sure we'll have time," Alex said. "Tomorrow."

"Gotta be now," Tony insisted. "It's very important stuff. It's about good ole Uncle Jase. He really messed up, and I mean big time."

What was the drunken fool talking about? Their uncle was long dead. Alex eased his brother down onto the bed and helped him take off his shoes. As he did, Tony rubbed his forehead and added, "Head's really pounding."

Alex nodded. "Hang on a second. I'll get you a washcloth."

He walked into the bathroom, ran a white washcloth under the cold water, and then wrung it out.

"Here you go," he said as he reentered the room.

But Tony was already asleep.

Alex loosened the top few buttons of his brother's shirt, pulled his tie off, and then covered him with a throw blanket.

As Alex started to leave, he remembered the key, and placed it on the dresser before he left.

"Good night, Tony," he said softly.

The only answer he got was a loud snore.

"My, he was a little tipsy, wasn't he?" Elise asked as Alex rejoined her a few minutes later.

"He was drunk. There's no reason to dance around it."

Elise nodded. "Okay, you're right. Sorry, I know you don't like things sugarcoated."

Alex shrugged. "Still want to marry me?"

She laughed. "Wait until you meet my Uncle Bobby. It's not really a party until he dances on the table and sings the Star Spangled Banner."

"That's not too bad."

"It might not be if he'd ever manage to keep his pants on while he was doing it," Elise said with a smile.

Alex had to laugh at the image, no matter how upset he was by his brother's visit. "So, we both have black sheep on our families."

"To say the least. He's here though, right? Isn't that all that really counts?"

"I suppose so," Alex said. "Though he didn't make a bit of sense upstairs."

"Did you expect him to?" Elise asked as one of the logs shifted in the fireplace.

Alex picked up an iron tool and shoved the burning wood back into place. "He said our uncle Jase messed up. I wonder if he even remembers that Jase is dead."

"Your brother clearly has his own share of demons to wrestle, doesn't he?"

Alex moved back to the couch, and stroked Elise's beautiful chestnut hair lightly. "You're really something, aren't you? After the way my brother has treated you in the past, you're still trying to give him the benefit of the doubt."

"Well, he's going to be a part of my family too, soon," she said.

He put an arm around her. "It's not soon enough for my taste. If we fly to Vegas tonight, we can get married tomorrow and skip all of this drama."

She laughed and pushed him away. "You want to get married in front of the lighthouse as much as I do, and I'm planning to just do this once. This is our home, Alex."

"I know, but you can't say you aren't at least a little tempted."

She grinned at him. "Okay, maybe a little." Elise yawned, and then said, "I should get some rest. Tomorrow's a big day. We've got folks coming in all day, then the rehearsal, the dinner afterwards, and finally the big day."

"At least our last guests left today," Alex said. "It's going to take some of the pressure off, not having any strangers staying here during the festivities. Are you sure we can afford to do it?"

She smiled at him. "Consider it a wedding present we are giving each other. I have a feeling our family and friends will be enough to handle without adding any outsiders into the mix, don't you?"

"I guess. I still think we should have shut the inn down completely and let them all fend for themselves."

She laughed. "What would you do with yourself if you didn't have the inn to run, even for a day? This is going to be perfect, trust me."

"I hope you're right."

"You know I am. Now, kiss me good night."

Alex was only too glad to follow that order.

As Elise started back for her room, she asked him, "Aren't you tired?"

He shrugged. "I've got to lock up, and then I might stay up with the fire for a while. I'll see you in the morning."

"Until then, my love," she said.

Alex was about to lock up when there was a light tap at the door. He considered ignoring it, and then saw that it was his best friend, Mor Pendleton. A former linebacker on his college football team, Mor had once had dreams of playing professional football, but those had ended with a knee injury. The scholarship, along with his college education, had ended with that blow, and Mor had come back to Elkton Falls. He didn't stay idle for long, though. He'd soon gone to work for Lester Williamson, and after a few years, the fix-it shop had become Mor or Les, a name everyone in Elkton Falls loved.

Mor had something in his hands, and when he held it up to the light, Alex saw that it was a large bottle of champagne, the same kind Alex had served at Mor's bachelor party. "Where did you get that?"

Mor grinned at him. "There's beer in the truck, too, but I figured since it was just the two of us, this would do."

Alex looked back at the door. "Where's Les? Isn't he coming?"

Mor shook his head. "He's feeling a little poorly these days."

Alex was alarmed by the news. He knew that his best friend's business partner was more than just a work associate to him. Lester had stepped in when Mor had needed him the most, and the two men were more like father and son than either one of them would ever admit. "Is it bad?"

"Who knows? The man is as tight lipped about his health as they come." He hoisted the bottle again. "Care for a sip?"

"Why not? I'm not driving anywhere tonight," Alex said.

"We could go up to the top of the lighthouse, if you'd like. That's what you did for me for my bachelor party."

Alex shook his head. "It's getting chilly, and we aren't exactly young men anymore. How's right here in front of the fire sound?"

"Like a real plan," Mor said.

"Hang on. I'll be right back," Alex said as he got a pair of glasses from the kitchen. As he returned, he handed one to Mor, he asked, "Where's your lovely bride tonight?"

Mor grimaced as he popped the cork and poured. "Where else would she be? She's working on your wedding. Since Elise asked her to lend a hand, the woman has become obsessed with decorations, arrangements, caterers, and anything else you could mention that might be even remotely related to your nuptials."

"And she didn't rope you into it all as well?"

Mor grinned. "I promised her that your bachelor party would be along the same lines as mine, and she was happy enough to let me go. To be honest with you, I think she was just looking for an excuse to get me out from underfoot."

Alex laughed. "I'll make sure you keep your word about my party."

Mor took a sip, and then put his glass down. Alex knew that his best friend was happier with root beer than champagne, but they were celebrating. The big man asked him softly, "Is your brother still coming in?"

"As a matter of fact, he's already here. He's upstairs right now."

"Should we invite him to join us?" Mor asked, though he wasn't fond of Alex's brother, and everyone in town knew it.

"No need. He's already drunk, so I don't think it's a good idea to pour any more liquor into him."

Mor shook his head. "Some brother you've got there."

Alex shrugged. "We can't pick our families, just our friends. Thanks for coming by tonight. I'd nearly forgotten all about having a bachelor party."

"Shoot, I should be thanking you. You got me out of wedding central."

As the two men sat by the fire, they chatted about old times, of the troubles, and the joys, they'd shared over the years. As far as Alex was concerned, it was the most fitting way to have a bachelor party he could think of.

Mor finally left, and Alex knocked down the last of the flames in the fireplace.

He glanced at his watch and saw that tomorrow would be there sooner than he liked.

As Alex drifted off to sleep, he wondered what his brother had been babbling about. He'd never been a particularly nice drunk, or all that well-meaning when he was sober, and Alex felt a little uncomfortable having him back at the inn.

Tony would be gone soon enough, though. After the wedding, he and Elise were going to shut down their inn to take a proper honeymoon, three days in Colonial Williamsburg, and then back home to run Hatteras West.

Alex couldn't wait for all of the fuss to be over so they could finally start the rest of their lives, together.

Chapter 3

Alex woke up and realized that this was the day before his wedding. It brought an immediate smile to his face, and he knew that no matter how bad the next two days might be, at the end of it, he and Elise would be husband and wife.

He came out of his room whistling, and found Elise already at the front desk. She was displaying a broad frown, and he wasn't sure how to handle it. Though he believed that he knew his bride-to-be well, Alex fully realized that his education up to that point had been somewhat lacking. He looked forward to getting to know her expressions and moods on a deeper level, but for now, he wasn't sure what to do. In a moment of spontaneity, he decided to give her a hug. After all, if he couldn't get her out of a bad mood today, he was in for some rough sailing in the future.

He walked in behind Elise, and then put his arms around her.

She turned to face him, and then buried her head into the nape of his neck. "How did you know? I really needed that," she said after she pulled away a full minute later.

"Heck, I was being selfish. I needed one myself. Why the frown before?"

She pointed to their registration book. "We have two couples booked for the Carolina Jasmine room the week we get back. We have got to get a better computer."

"Pick one out. We'll find a way to pay for it." Alex had a sudden thought. "Hey, maybe we'll get some cash as a wedding present. We could use it for that."

She nodded with a smile. "What a great idea. That sounds perfect."

He hugged her again. "Elise, I'm just glad you're so flexible. I don't know what I would do if you were the type of person who expected to be spoiled all of the time," he said.

"Oh, I do. I insist on laughter, hugs, kisses, and you being here, instead of anything more material. As far as I'm concerned, the rest is just icing on the cake."

"By the way, how's the cake coming?" Alex knew that Irma Bean from Mama Ravolini's was taking care of their wedding cake, and she'd promised them something extraordinary. Alex wasn't all that sure how unique their cake needed to be, but he'd kept his nose out of it.

"It's going well. Irma and I had a long chat about what we want, and Emma's riding herd over her, so I'm not worried about it."

"She's taking on a lot, isn't she? Mor was here last night after you went to bed. During my bachelor party, he told me how hard she's been working lately."

"She insisted, but I'm taking up some of the slack." Elise looked at him and smiled. "Your get-together must not have been too wild. I didn't even hear you."

"We were quietly celebrating," Alex said with a grin of his own. "I don't get the whole last chance to be single idea, anyway. I can't imagine anything more exciting than being with you." He wasn't all that prone to declarations about his feelings like that, but if a man couldn't say those things on the eve of his own wedding, maybe he shouldn't be getting married at all.

Alex looked at Elise, and noticed a tear tracking down her cheek. "Did I say something wrong?" he asked.

"No, I don't know what's gotten into me. I'm weepy all of a sudden, and I've never been that way in my life up until now."

"Hey, we're both happy. Let's just leave it at that. Everything set for the rehearsal dinner tonight, or do I need to touch base with Monet's Garden?"

"No worries, Alex, it's all under control."

"Good," Alex said. "What's left for me to do?"

She grinned at him. "I was hoping you'd ask. Shantara called, and she got in that door-lock we've been waiting for. Why don't you take the truck and run into town?"

"You're not trying to get me out from underfoot, are you?"

Elise pretended to be astonished. "Me? I wouldn't dream of it."

He kissed her, and they both laughed. "I'll be back later."

"See you for lunch," Elise said.

Alex got into his ancient pickup and headed into Elkton Falls. Shantara Robinson was a long-time friend of his. She ran the general store in town, inheriting it from her father about the same time that Alex's own parents had died and left him and his brother the lighthouse inn, cash and securities, and a handful of stocks. Alex, in a moment he never, or rarely ever, regretted, had offered Tony everything he'd inherited for his share of the lighthouse property, and his brother, always driven by greed, had readily agreed. Even growing up, Tony had never had any use for the lighthouse, something he'd always considered an oddity and an embarrassment instead of a delight.

Alex picked up the door-lock, spent a little time browsing the aisles of the store, drove around town a little, and basically just killed time until he had to meet back up with Elise. The errand had another benefit as well. Alex didn't have to see his brother, at least not soon. Why couldn't they get along? Alex had made every effort over the years, but Tony hadn't been interested.

He was in Elkton Falls now, though, and Alex resolved to make one last stab at getting along with his brother. They were adults; surely they could put childhood slights and fights behind them for what was the happiest time of Alex's life.

As Alex drove up to the inn, he found his brother sitting on the lighthouse's front steps.

Tony waved to him, and Alex decided there was no time like the present to start patching things up.

"Where did you run off to?" Tony asked, the ire thick in his voice. "I've been looking all over the place for you all morning."

"I had to run into town on an errand. What's going on?"

"We need to talk," Tony said.

From the angry tone in his brother's voice, Alex knew that this might not be the best time to work things out. "I've got to get inside. Can we do it later?"

Tony was about to protest when Elise called out from the steps of the Dual Keepers' Quarters. "Lunch, guys. Come on in."

"Hang on a second," Alex called out, and then turned back to his brother. He might as well get it over with. "What is it?"

"It'll keep till later," Tony said with a frown.

"Good," Alex answered. Delaying this particular conversation was fine with him.

As the two of them walked back toward the inn, Alex asked, "How long are you staying in Elkton Falls?"

"Maybe for quite a while," Tony said, shocking Alex with his reply.

"Really? That's great," Alex answered, trying to mean what he said. "Any reason in particular?"

Tony just smiled, but there was something about it that Alex didn't like.

He didn't have long to think about it, though. When he got to Elise, he could see that she'd been crying.

"What's wrong? Did something happen? Are your folks okay?"

"As far as I know," she said.

Tony butted in. "I'll see you inside."

After he left, they were alone. "Go on, you can tell me."

"Irma called. There's an issue with the cake."

"That's a relief," Alex said. "I thought it was something important."

"You don't think our wedding cake is important?" she asked with a hint of anger in her voice.

"Hey, I'm one of the good guys, remember? What is it? Between the two of us, we'll fix it."

"I'm sure the cake will be fine, if I want to be a widow as soon as I'm a bride."

"What do you mean?" Alex asked.

"The batter she used was coconut. You're allergic."

"Trust me, I'm not about to forget." He thought about it, and then shrugged. "I can't eat it, but that doesn't mean everyone else can't enjoy it."

"Alex Winston, if you think for one second that we're going to have a wedding cake that my new husband can't eat, you've lost your mind."

"So, she can make us another one." It seemed simple enough to Alex.

"In one day? It's impossible."

He wrapped her up in another hug. "Nothing else matters except saying 'I do' to you."

She bit her lower lip, and then said, "You're right. I just wanted everything to be perfect."

He held her tightly, and then said, "It is. 'I do,' remember?"

She laughed at him. "You're right. It's not that big a deal. She can make another cake. It won't be as nice as the one I ordered, but at least it won't kill you."

"I'm all for that," Alex said with a grin. "Has anything else gone wrong today yet?"

She smiled at him. "No, I don't have any more problems scheduled until after lunch."

"Sounds good to me," he said.

"Then let's eat. I'm starving."

"Is this when I say 'I do'?" Alex asked the preacher as he and Elise stood on the lighthouse steps late in the afternoon.

"Yes, but save it for later," Kyle said. "We don't want to jump the gun, do we?"

Alex answered without thinking, "Speak for yourself, John Alden."

Everyone gathered there laughed, including Elise. She

squeezed his hand, and as they finished the rehearsal, Alex couldn't keep the broad grin off of his face. He looked over at Elise's parents, and was still taken aback from being quietly asked before the rehearsal to call them Mom and Dad after the ceremony. Alex had lost his own parents long ago, and that touching gesture had nearly made him cry.

Alex turned to the crowd, including his brother, who was standing quite a bit away from the lighthouse, and called out, "We're meeting at Monet's Garden for dinner, so if you need a ride, find somebody here. We'll see you all there."

Alex steered Elise toward his truck. "Do you mind riding with me in this?"

"I'm happy to," Elise said. As he held the door for her, she slid across the seat and was waiting for him when he got in. As Elise belted in beside him, she put her head on his shoulder. "I've been waiting all day for this."

"What, a ride in my rusty old chariot?" he asked with a grin. She was wearing a pale green dress that showed off her figure, and her chestnut hair was put up and arranged in some kind of fancy styling that made her look like a princess to him, not that he didn't feel that way about her all of the time. His suit was uncomfortable, but then again, it would have been hard to beat his blue jeans and one of his faded old flannel shirts that he loved wearing. If he were being honest about it, it was what he preferred to see Elise in as well. Dressed like this, with her hair done and makeup skillfully applied, she looked unattainable to him, somehow. It was only in blue jeans and one of his old shirts that he realized just how lucky he was.

Elise touched his cheek lightly. "What are you thinking about, Alex?"

"How much I love you in jeans," he answered without thinking about it. "Not that you aren't beautiful now, because you are. I don't know what I'm trying to say. Forgive me."

She laughed out loud, with no reserve. "Are you kidding? That's one of the things I love most about you.

Peter always insisted that I get dressed up to go to the grocery store. He hated seeing me in blue jeans."

"Then that's just one more way the man was a fool for letting you go," Alex said.

In a meek voice, Elise said, "He called the inn today."

"What?" Alex asked, shocked at the news. Peter had followed Elise to North Carolina when she'd taken the job at Hatteras West, but that was a long time ago. "What did he want?"

"He said he wanted to congratulate me on our wedding," Elise said.

Alex grunted. "The idiot should be congratulating me, not you."

"Why's that?"

"You aren't the one getting the prize," Alex said.

"There, you're wrong," she replied. "I'm every bit as lucky as you are."

"Is that all he wanted?" Alex asked, not able to help himself. He had a sore spot when it came to the man, and he knew it. Asheford was handsome, and rich to boot, and Alex always felt a little less than he was when he was around Asheford.

"He asked me if I was happy," Elise admitted.

"He was probably hoping you would change your mind about marrying me," Alex said, trying to lighten the mood a little.

She looked at him quizzically. "Yes, that's it, exactly. How did you know?"

"I guessed, but it's not that hard a leap to make. What did you say?"

She squeezed his arm. "That for the first time in my life, I'm truly in love, and that I wouldn't give that up for anything."

"If I weren't driving right now, I'd kiss you."

"If you weren't driving, I'd encourage it."

They both laughed, and the tension was eased again between them.

When Alex and Elise got to Monet's Garden, the parking lot was full. Alex hoped that their rehearsal dinner wouldn't get swallowed up whatever else was going on there, but they'd asked for a private dining area, so hopefully it would be all right.

As they walked in the door, they saw a great many more folks than the wedding party and a few out of town guests waiting for them as well.

"Surprise," they all shouted, and Alex looked quizzically at Elise. "Did you know about this?"

"I'm as baffled as you are," Elise said.

Monet himself, the restaurant's owner and namesake, approached them. "Welcome, my friends. I haven't forgotten what you did for me when I first opened, and I hope you will allow me to repay you by hosting this surprise dinner. You approve?"

Elise squeezed Alex's hand as she said, "Of course we do, but you shouldn't have gone to all of this trouble."

"No trouble at all. Now come, enjoy yourselves. The restaurant is yours, and yours alone, this evening. Consider it my wedding present to the two of you."

Alex could only imagine what the gesture was costing his friend, but he was resolved to graciously accept it. "Thank you," Alex said as he shook the man's hand heartily.

"Thank you," Elise echoed, and then kissed Monet on the cheek.

Monet looked happy enough to burst. He clapped his hands together, and then said, "Let the festivities begin!"

Alex was suddenly awash with old friends, and even some guests from the inn who had become a part of his circle over the years. Evans Graile, a sprightly older man, approached them with a present in his hands.

"It's good to see you, Evans," Alex said.

"I was overjoyed to get the invitation tonight." He extended the present he'd been holding toward them. "I just want to wish you both much happiness."

"There's a table for presents by the door," Emma Sturbridge said as she approached them.

"I'll put it there, then," Evans said. "It's the most wonderful single serving tea brewer and a medley of exotic teas. I hope you like it."

Alex tried not to laugh. Evans Graile wasn't devoted to much in the world, but he loved his teas, and he tried to share that affection with the rest of the world whenever he could.

"It's perfect," Elise said as she smiled at him.

Emma led Evans away, but there was no respite from the crowd. Next in line was Buck and his daughter, Sally Anne, both from Buck's Grill.

Buck, a large man who had once been a boxer, slapped Alex on the shoulder. "Knew you'd finally get around to pulling the trigger," Buck said.

"Dad," Sally Anne protested, "Everyone can hear you."

"I'm not ashamed of what I said," Buck said. "Our present's on the pile."

Sally Anne started to protest, but Elise touched her hand lightly. "Thank you both so much for coming."

"We wouldn't have missed it," Sally Anne said.

There was a disturbance at the front door, and Alex saw a shifty looking man having an argument with his brother. He excused himself, and then walked over to them and said, "Is there a problem?"

"No problem at all," Tony said a little too quickly.

"That's a matter of interpretation," the man said.

"Jackson, we'll talk later."

"Sooner, I think," the man said, but he finally walked away.

"What was that all about?" Alex asked.

"Nothing you need to worry about," Tony answered.

Alex was about to rejoin Elise when a woman approached Tony and slapped him hard across the face. She said, "If you think you're getting away with this, you're dead wrong."

Before Tony could reply, she stormed out the door,

slamming it just as a flash of lightning hit.

"Try not to wreck this for me," Alex said to Tony as thunder rumbled.

As he rejoined Elise, she asked, "What was that all about?"

"I'll tell you later," Alex replied as Sheriff Armstrong, his sometime nemesis when it came to solving crimes around Elkton Falls, approached. The sheriff was in a suit, looking oddly out of place out of uniform. He nodded to Alex and Elise, and then said, "Congrats, you two."

"Thanks, Sheriff. Glad you could make it."

He shrugged. "Everybody else in town is here. Somebody has to keep the peace." As he said it, he glanced over at Alex's brother.

There was no way Alex was going to let himself get dragged into that. There was only one way to respond to that, and that was with humor. Alex grinned. "If a riot breaks out, I'll lend you a hand myself."

Armstrong shrugged without commenting, and then walked away.

Elise scolded Alex. "You shouldn't have teased him like that."

"If I get the chance, I'm never passing it up," Alex said with a big grin.

Elise started to say something else, but before she could, Doc Drake and his wife, and nurse, Madge, approached. "What did you say to him, Alex?" his friend, the doctor, asked.

"I offered to volunteer my services for crowd control if he needed me," Alex explained.

The doctor began to smile, and Madge said, "You two are quite the pair, aren't you?"

Alex looked at the doctor, and they both smiled. "We like to think so."

Madge laughed, but checked it slightly as she looked at Elise. "Are you sure you know what you're getting yourself into?"

"My eyes are wide open. Trust me, I have no delusions about the man I'm marrying."

"Hey, I'm standing right here," Alex said.

As he spoke, another flash of lightning was quickly followed by a long rumble of thunder that filled the air.

Alex saw the concerned look on Elise's face. "Don't worry. If it rains tomorrow, we can get married in the main lobby."

"I know, but it's not the lighthouse, is it?"

Madge smiled at them. "You two are the perfect match. Alex, I don't know how you managed to find someone as crazy about that lighthouse as you are, but you'd better be good to her."

"That's a promise I'll have no trouble keeping," Alex said. The rain began in earnest then, and they could hear it beating down on the restaurant's roof.

Alex was determined not to let it spoil the mood of the evening, though.

He was getting married tomorrow, and nothing else mattered.

Or so he thought.

Chapter 4

Back at the inn, everyone was settled in for the night, but Alex couldn't get to sleep, no matter how hard he tried. He'd been avoiding Tony all evening since the pair of confrontations he'd witnessed, hoping that whatever his brother had to say to him could wait, but when Alex walked out onto the porch, he found his brother there, sitting in the shadows. At least the rain had finally stopped.

"I figured you'd come out here eventually," Tony said.

"I was just going to bed," Alex said.

"Alex, I hate to rain on your parade, but you need to hear this before you get married. It's going to affect your life, and you need to make sure Elise knows what she's getting herself into."

He had had enough of his brother. "What is it, Tony?"

"It's all of this," Alex's brother said as he waved a hand around the air.

"What are you talking about?"

"Uncle Jase made a mistake when he wrote up the transfer of property when we settled the estate. It's invalid, Alex. I had an attorney look it over, and there are issues with the agreement that make it unenforceable."

Alex couldn't believe what he was hearing. "What are you talking about, Tony? Why did you have a lawyer involved in the first place?"

"Hey, fair is fair," Tony protested. "Family is one thing, but legal is another."

Alex reached down and grabbed his brother's shirt roughly just as someone walked out onto the porch. It was Alex's future father-in-law.

"Is there a problem here?" Mr. Danton asked Alex pointedly.

Alex released his brother's shirt. "No problem, sir. Just

two brothers having a little chat."

Elise's father looked skeptical, but he kept it to himself. "I'll just turn in, then."

"You're lucky he saved you," Tony said after Elise's father was gone. "It would be tough getting arrested for assault on the day before you were supposed to get married."

"Tony, I gave you everything, all the stocks, the bank accounts, the insurance money, just so I could keep the inn. What happened to all of that money?"

"It's gone," Tony said.

"So you started looking around for another easy score, didn't you? Well, it's not going to be that simple. This place is mine."

"Not according to my attorney."

Alex couldn't believe this was happening. It was the stuff of the worst nightmares he'd ever had in his life. "We agreed. You took that money."

"Listen, I don't want to take this place from you. Give me a hundred thousand right now, and we'll call it even."

Alex couldn't keep from laughing, despite the tragedy of the discussion. "Tony, I could barely scrape up a tenth of that if I cashed in everything liquid I have, including any wedding money Elise and I may or may not get tomorrow."

Tony frowned. "I don't believe you. This place has to be making money. Don't jerk me around, Alex. This is a one time offer, good until midnight tonight. You've got it, and you know it."

"I can show you my checkbook if it will prove it to you. We need a new boiler, our air conditioning system is nearly shot, and the lighthouse needs to be painted. For all intents and purposes, I'm broke, and steadily going deeper in the hole every day."

"How about fifty thousand?" Tony asked. "I'm willing to be reasonable about it."

"How about nothing," Alex said, his temper getting the better of him.

"Then get ready to sell this place, dear brother, because if you can't pay up, I want half the cash value for what this whole thing is worth. You can kiss your lighthouse good bye, Alex."

And before Alex could say another word, Tony walked off the porch and into the night.

Alex didn't know what to do next, but his instincts were strong. He found himself walking toward Elise's room without realizing that was where he was headed. He needed to talk about what had just happened, and there was no one in the world he'd rather discuss it with than Elise.

Alex knocked on the door of her room. "Elise, it's Alex."

He heard her voice from the other side of the door. "What is it, Alex? It's late."

"Something's wrong," he said.

That was all it took. "Give me one minute," she said.

Alex slumped down on a chair in the hallway and waited for her. He knew his brother was capable of some atrocious things, but trying to extort money out of him after taking so much was even beyond his low standards. Someone was putting pressure on Tony for money, and fast; that much was obvious. But Alex wasn't going to roll over and just give it to him.

Elise came out wearing blue jeans and an old t shirt. Her hair was pulled back into a ponytail, she had no makeup on at all; Alex had never seen her more beautiful.

"What's wrong?"

"Tony. He claims there was something wrong with the transfer Uncle Jase drew up between us when our folks died."

"What does that mean, exactly?"

Alex could barely force the words out of his mouth. "He says we have to sell Hatteras West."

"We need some coffee," Elise said as she led him into the lobby.

As they walked down the hallway into the main area,

Elise said, "I don't care what time it is. You have to call Sandra."

Sandra Beckett was Alex's attorney, and one-time girlfriend.

"It's late," Alex said.

"I don't think she'll mind. Call her, Alex. She'll know what to do."

Alex nodded, willing to do whatever Elise suggested to make this nightmare go away. He looked up Sandra's home number, and after seven rings, she picked up.

"Did I wake you?" Alex asked.

"Alex, is that you? Of course not. I was going over some paperwork. What's wrong? You're not drunk, are you?"

"What? No, of course not. Why would you ask that?"

There was a pause, and then Sandra said, "You hear stories about bridegrooms with cold feet all of the time. They call old girlfriends when their weddings get close at hand."

"No worries about me. My toes have never been toastier," Alex said.

"Then why the call?"

"I have a serious legal problem, and I need your advice," he replied.

"Nobody's dead, are they?"

Alex couldn't believe the questions Sandra was asking. "No, no one's dead."

"Hey, you can't blame me for asking. That lighthouse of yours seems to attract its share of dead bodies. If it's not that, what is it?"

"My brother claims that the document transferring his share of the lighthouse to me isn't valid. He's saying that we'll have to sell everything."

Sandra whistled softly. "No wonder you called. Alex, did Jase draw up the transfer?"

Alex said, "Yes, of course he did. He was a good attorney."

"Hey, I loved that man like a father, but we both know how torn up he was about your parents' accident. He wasn't on his game, and he knew it. Jase ran things past me for two months after they died, but I never saw that transfer."

Alex felt the wind go out of his lungs. Could Tony be telling the truth?

His thoughts were interrupted when Sandra added, "If you have the document, I'll be glad to take a look at it. I can be there in fifteen minutes."

"It's in my safety deposit box at the bank," Alex admitted. "I won't be able to get it out for two days."

Sandra said, "That's convenient, isn't it?"

"If you ask me, it's exactly the opposite."

"Stay with me. Did Tony offer some kind of cash settlement, something that had to be done immediately?"

Alex bit his lip. "He said he'd take a hundred grand, but it had to be before the wedding. As a matter of fact, when I turned him down, he cut that in half, not that I have a prayer of paying either amount."

Sandra paused for a moment, and then said, "Take my advice. Don't give him a dime, Alex."

"Why not?" he asked.

"I think he's bluffing, but even if he's not, I'll represent you in this. We can show that Tony took your share of the inheritance, and you signed that document in good faith. I think we have a case, even if Jase did drop the ball. Try not to worry about it, okay?"

"I don't see how, but thanks, Sandra."

"I'll see you tomorrow at the wedding," she said, and then hung up.

Elise had been listening to his side of the conversation, and Alex had held the phone off from his ear far enough for her to pick up most of what Sandra had said.

"That's a relief, isn't it?" Elise said.

"I guess," Alex admitted. "Don't think this is going to go away, though. I know my brother. He'll try his best to break us with a lawsuit. This is going to cost me a fortune."

"You're wrong, there," Elise said softly.

Alex asked, "What, you think Sandra is going to do this for free?"

"No, but we'll pay for it together. I have some money I've been saving that I wanted to surprise you with. I was going to buy us a new boiler, but this is more important."

"Elise, I can't take your money," Alex said, almost reflexively.

"Listen, and listen good, Alex Winston. As of tomorrow night, there is no more 'mine' and 'yours'. It's all ours, the good and the bad. Do you understand me?"

"I do," he said.

She laughed. "Good. Keep repeating that, and when the preacher asks you tomorrow, remember your line."

He kissed her, and after a few moments, Elise said, "Thanks for the good night kiss."

"Thank you for being here," Alex said.

Sandra and Elise didn't seem nearly as worried about the situation as Alex was, but then they hadn't grown up at Hatteras West. He wasn't at all surprised that his brother had tried to cheat him.

And that by itself was a sad thing indeed.

Alex woke up just past one am, and it took him a second to realize that the sound of the front door of the inn slamming hadn't been a part of some kind of dream. He was so attuned to the sounds of the inn, the whispers and moans of the building, that he could tell whenever something was not as it should be. Throwing on a robe, he walked out into the lobby, turning lights on along the way.

Nothing looked out of place as he searched the space, but as Alex walked to the door, he felt his heart drop.

It hadn't been a dream. It was unlocked.

Had he forgotten to lock it last night, given all that had happened? Alex thought his routines were so ingrained that he could have done them in his sleep, but apparently, the news Tony had dropped on him the night before had thrown him off his game.

There was another option, though. What if someone staying upstairs had left abruptly in the middle of the night? His thoughts immediately went to Tony.

"Alex, what is it?"

"Sorry if that woke you," he told Elise.

"Then that wasn't you slamming the door a minute ago?" she asked.

"No, I heard it, too, so I decided to come out and investigate." He looked back up the stairs. "Should we wake everyone up and do a head count?"

Elise shook her head. "We could check the hallway, but I don't want to wake my folks up unless there's a good reason."

"Agreed," Alex said.

He started up the steps to their guest rooms, glad that the Main Keeper's Quarters was empty. At least anything that happened would be contained in this building. Having two separate structures that housed their guests was a pain at times, but he hadn't laid out the inn, his ancestors had, so he had to live with it.

Everything looked normal upstairs. At least that was something.

"Maybe it just was the wind," Elise said.

"Blowing through the lobby outside? Someone slammed that door, Elise."

He lingered at his brother's door, hesitating for a moment.

Elise asked, "Alex, you aren't going to wake him, are you?"

"I have a feeling he's not there," Alex said. He knocked on the door, once, twice, and a third time before he took his keys out of his robe pocket.

"Are you going inside?"

"I need to know if he's there," Alex said. "I've got a bad feeling about this."

Alex opened the door, feeling his hand shake a little as he

nearly fumbled the key. When Alex threw the door opened, he half expected to see something tragic there.

When he realized that nothing was amiss, not in the room or the bathroom, he let out a breath he hadn't even realized that he'd been holding.

"Nothing," he reported back to Elise, who had lingered in the hallway.

"That's good news, isn't it?"

"His bed hasn't been slept in," Alex said, "and his suitcase is gone. It appears that my brother came to deliver his ultimatum, and then left."

Elise touched his shoulder lightly. "I'm so sorry, Alex."

"Don't be," Alex said. "I wouldn't expect anything less from my brother." He glanced at the clock in the hallway. "We need to get some rest. After all, we've got a big day tomorrow."

"Today, actually," Elise said with a grin. "But honestly, I'm wide awake. How about a cup of hot chocolate?"

"You twisted my arm," he said. Alex sat and watched her make the cocoa, and the two of them moved into the lobby and lit another fire. As they sat there, they talked about their time together at Hatteras West and their plans for the future. The time flew past, and Alex realized that if they didn't get some sleep soon, it would be too late to get any. And they had a big day ahead of them.

At 3:00 am, they said their final good nights as two single people, and went their separate ways. Alex had a little trouble falling back to sleep. Though he wasn't surprised by his brother's hasty exit, he was a little disappointed. If Tony had stayed around, Alex might have had a chance to talk him out of the lawsuit, but as things stood, there wasn't a prayer of that happening now.

It put a huge damper on what should have been a joyous occasion, but there was nothing he could do about it.

Elise had made her stance clear.

No matter what happened, they were going to get married

today.

And with that bright note, Alex finally managed to drift off to sleep.

Chapter 5

"You look like a wreck," Mor told Alex the next afternoon. Alex knew that Elise and Emma had conspired to keep his mind off the impending nuptials, and had enlisted his best friend to keep him occupied.

"I told you, I didn't get much sleep last night."

"Nervous about the big day? I was so scared I stayed up all night wondering if I was doing the right thing."

"And what have you discovered since you married Emma?"

Mor grinned at him. "That it was the best thing that ever happened to me. Don't worry about it, cold feet are expected."

"If anything, I can't wait to get married."

"Then why the trouble sleeping?"

"Elise and I heard a door slam last night, and after we investigated, we saw that Tony was gone. We couldn't get back to sleep, so we stayed up and drank hot chocolate in front of the fire until late."

"You're right, you do belong with Elise. Sorry I wore you out today." The two men had hiked around Bear Rocks, gone for a drive, and were now checking the rooms in the empty Main Keeper's Quarters for something they could fix.

"Are you kidding? The distraction was exactly what I needed."

"Good. Now, what can we do here at the inn? How about the light switches? Are they all in working order?" Mor asked as he hefted his toolbox on their quest for something meaningful to do.

"You don't have to do this," Alex said.

Mor grinned at him. "Are you kidding me? This helps me out in two ways. I didn't know what to get you as a wedding present, so a free day of work from Les and me was Elise's suggestion. That's one practical woman you've got there."

"What's the second reason?"

"My wife won't be trying to dragoon me into her wedding prep squad." Mor patted Alex hard on the back. "It's a win-win situation no matter how I look at it."

"Well, if you're sure, there's a closet light in the Blue Ridge Suite that never has worked."

"Let's see to it, then," Mor said.

Alex opened the door, and Mor walked over to the closet. He flipped the switch, and nothing happened. After a moment, he pulled off the cover plate, looked in, and said, "I can fix this in two seconds."

"Should I turn off the power?" Alex asked.

"No, it's okay. I'm fine."

Mor worked for five minutes, and when he was finished, the light came right on at the flick of the switch.

"That's great," Alex said.

"Anything else in here need fixing?" Mor asked.

"I don't think so."

Mor took out his outlet tester and said, "Let's check anyway."

"They all work," Alex said.

Mor plugged the tester into an outlet behind the door. "This one's dead."

"It can't be. It was working last week when I vacuumed here."

"Maybe it was tied in with the switch," Mor said.

"Is that even possible?"

"With this old wiring, nothing would surprise me. Let's see what we've got," Mor said as he started to take the cover plate off.

"I really should turn the electricity off." As an innkeeper, Alex was a jack of most trades, but he wasn't all that comfortable when it came to two things: electricity, and natural gas lines.

"If I have to swap it out with another receptacle, we'll kill it, but I'm just looking right now."

Mor took out a large flashlight and peered into the outlet as soon as it was exposed.

"That's odd," he said.

"What? Did a wire slip off?"

"From what I can see, the wires aren't even connected to this outlet at all." He took his screwdriver and began to remove the outlet itself.

"Well, would you look at that," he said.

The big man was blocking his view, so Alex couldn't see anything at all. "What is it?"

"This outlet was live pretty recently, but someone's taped off the wires and killed the outlet on purpose."

"How can you tell?"

"The electrical tape looks brand new, and the scratches on the posts look fresh."

Alex had to take his friend's word on that. "Why would anyone do that?"

"Beats me." Mor reached into the opening, and Alex was afraid his friend would get a shock despite the protected wires, but instead, he pulled out a small folded piece of paper.

"What is it?" Alex asked.

"I figure it's your inn. You should have the honors. It's probably a gag by a disgruntled electrician."

"It could be," Alex said.

As he opened the paper, Alex found a cryptic photocopy, of what, Alex was not at all sure. There were what appeared to be random numbers in several columns, but they made no sense at all to him.

He showed Mor, who examined it as well, but the big man couldn't make out any meaning to it, either.

"I have no idea why anyone would do that," Mor said. "I need a drink of water."

Alex was still studying the fragment when Mor called out from the bathroom, "Alex, get in here."

"Hang on a second," Alex said, still trying to figure out what the piece of paper could mean.

"I don't have a second. Then again, maybe you should stay right where you are."

That got Alex's attention. He started for the bathroom door, but Mor blocked the way.

"What is it?" Alex asked, a fresh sense of urgency in his voice.

"You don't need to see this." He shoved his cell phone into Alex's hands. "Call Armstrong."

Alex felt his body go numb. "Is it Elise?" He couldn't imagine living without her, and wasn't sure he'd even want to.

"No, it's not her. It's Tony." Mor could barely get out the next few words. "I'm sorry. He's dead."

Alex looked at his friend to see if it was some kind of twisted joke, but one glance at Mor's expression told him that this was no laughing matter.

"I need to see him," Alex said.

"You shouldn't. Trust me."

Alex pushed his big friend aside, something that he wouldn't have said was possible if he hadn't just done it.

Tony was lying in the tub, face up, with a knife plunged into his chest.

It was clear there was no life left him.

"It's not a joke, is it?" Alex asked, still not able to believe what he was seeing. "Could he be trying to pull a prank on me on Halloween?"

Mor shook his head. "The blood is real, there's no pulse, and he's as cold as can be. I don't know how long he's been dead, but it's been awhile."

Alex nodded, but he still had to see for himself. The bathmat was gone, so he knelt beside the body on the cold tile and studied his brother for a second from close up.

"He's gone, Alex," Mor said gently, as though he were informing Alex that it was raining outside. Alex ignored it, and his fingers probed for a pulse. Mor was right. Tony had been dead awhile. His skin was cold to the touch, as though the late October air had sucked out every last bit of warmth he'd had in him. It felt to Alex as though some kind of weird transference took place just then. It was almost as if Tony's body was beginning to chill him as well. Alex pulled his hand away, and started to get up, putting his hand on the side of the tub for support.

Mor helped him up. "Are you okay?"

Alex just nodded as he suddenly realized that he was the last living Winston in his branch of the family tree.

Mor guided him gently back out of the room, and he tried to take his phone back from Alex. "I'll call the sheriff."

"No, I can handle it myself," he said.

"Sheriff, this is Alex Winston," he said once he got the sheriff on the phone. It had taken three minutes, with each passing second feeling as though it lasted a lifetime. From where he stood, Alex could see that the hardwood floor was scuffed, and he strangely thought that he and Elise should buff it out before the police came. He knew on one level that it made no sense, but he wasn't in his best frame of mind, either. The drapes needed to be replaced as well, he thought to himself.

Sheriff Armstrong finally came on the line. "What's going on, Alex? The wedding's still happening, right? You didn't cancel it, did you?"

Was the sheriff trying to make a joke? Alex suddenly realized that it was true. There was no way he and Elise could be married, at least not now.

"Not yet, but we have to. Somebody killed my brother at the inn."

"Are you serious?" the sheriff asked.

"As I can be," Alex admitted.

"You know the drill. Don't touch anything. I'll be right there." The sheriff hesitated a moment, and then said, "Alex, I'm sorry, about your brother, and the wedding."

"Thanks," he said. "Mor will be guarding the door when you get here. Come to the Main Keeper's Quarters."

"Where will you be?"

"I have to tell Elise that the wedding's off."

Alex found Elise in the kitchen, helping Emma with the birdseed packets folks would have been throwing at them after the ceremony. The women were laughing and smiling as Alex came in.

Elise dropped the packet she was tying with ribbon and rushed to Alex. She must have read something in his face. "What's wrong?"

"Tony's been murdered," Alex said. "We have to call the wedding off."

Elise looked as though she couldn't believe it. "What? Tell me again, but give me details."

Emma asked, "Where's Mor?"

"He's guarding the body over at the Main Keepers Quarters until the sheriff gets here."

"Then that's where I need to be," Emma said.

"You shouldn't do that," Alex said.

Emma didn't even slow down, though. Her place was with her husband, and there was no way anyone would be able to keep her from joining him.

Alex slumped down in a chair after Emma was gone.

"I'm so sorry, Alex," Elise said as she stroked his hair lightly. "I know you two had your problems, but he was your brother."

"I can't believe this is happening. Elise, you know how much I love you, how much you mean to me, but we can't do this, not now."

Elise shushed him. "Of course not. After we find the killer, we'll have our wedding ceremony, but Alex, in my heart, we're already married. All that's left are the formalities."

"What about the honeymoon?" Alex asked.

Elise shook her head. "We'll have to cancel that, too."

"It's already paid for. We can't get a refund, but we can transfer it to someone else." Alex had a sudden idea. As he stood, he asked, "Why don't we give it to your parents? You said yourself they need a vacation more than anything in the world. Let's send them instead."

"Alex, we don't have to talk about that right now."

"Elise, there's nothing to talk about. It's settled. Go tell them."

She hugged him tightly. "You continue to prove to me that I've found the right man to spend the rest of my life back. They are as frugal as we are. I'll tell them the trip is nonrefundable, and they'll have to go. Thank you, Alex, that means so much to me."

"You should go tell them," he said.

"I can do that later. Right now, you need me."

"Elise, I love you with all my heart, but I need a bit of time alone to come to grips with this. I'm going to climb to the top of the lighthouse and see if I can make any sense of it. Do you mind?"

"I knew she'd be your mistress long after I became your wife," Elise said with a smile. "Don't worry, I love her too, and I'm not the jealous type."

Elise walked Alex to the foot of the lighthouse, and as Alex passed by the first window, he saw her going back inside.

He doubted that many people would have understood his bond to the lighthouse, and his need to be alone atop it.

He'd found the right person, too.

"Alex, are you up there?" he heard a voice call out from below the tower. "I need to talk to you."

Alex peered over the walkway and saw the sheriff standing far below. "You could just come up."

"Not likely. Let's go, this is serious."

Alex considered a hundred things he could say in reply, but there was no use. He hurried down the steps, and found the sheriff waiting for him at the bottom.

"We need to talk."

Alex nodded. "I guess you heard about the fight Tony and I had last night," Alex said.

"Mor mentioned it." Alex had brought his friend up to

date on the phone about Tony's threat to take half the lighthouse, so it didn't surprise him." He wasn't trying to rat you out, Alex. He just didn't want me to find out on my own."

"I've never doubted Mor's loyalty to me, Sheriff, and I'm not about to start now. I wasn't all that pleased with my brother, but I didn't kill him."

"That's what we need to talk about," Armstrong said. The sheriff looked at the ground for a moment, and then said, "I just spoke with your father-in-law."

"He's not going to have that title for awhile," Alex said, and then it hit him. "He told you about last night on the porch, didn't he?"

The sheriff nodded. "He didn't want to at first, but his wife insisted. They aren't bad people, Alex. They just want to be sure their daughter is marrying the right man. You can't hold it against them."

"I don't," Alex said, though in truth he wasn't pleased by the news. What did he expect, though? If he'd been in Mr. Danton's shoes and it was his daughter getting married, wouldn't he speak up? Of course he would. Elise's parents clearly loved her, and if they thought there was a single chance she was getting herself into some serious trouble, they were obligated to speak up.

"You mean that?" Armstrong asked. "I'm not sure I'd be so forgiving, myself."

"What if it was your daughter getting married?" he asked simply.

The sheriff didn't take long to consider the possibilities. "I'd rat you out in a second."

"The thing is, I didn't kill Tony."

"But he was threatening all of this," the sheriff said as he waved a hand around the place. Alex had often thought of the man as nothing more than a blundering fool, but in fact, Armstrong had changed since the heart attack he'd had while Alex and Elise were away working on the Outer Banks at another lighthouse inn. It was as though God had given him another chance, and he'd decided to grab it with both hands. It didn't mean that he and Alex could ever be considered friends, but the sheriff wasn't as quick to think Alex committed a crime as he had in the past.

"That's a point, but I spoke with Sandra Beckett last night, and she promised me she'd have my back, that Tony didn't have a leg to stand on."

"It's kind of crazy how you two have stayed friends, even after you dumped her for Elise."

"There was a little difference of opinion in the timing of it all," Alex said. "But I trust Sandra, and so does Elise."

The sheriff nodded. "Okay, we know why you might have wanted to see your brother dead. Have any other suspects I can look at?"

Alex nodded. At least he wasn't being led off to jail, at least not yet. "You should speak with two people who were at the rehearsal dinner last night. Remember the woman who slapped Tony?"

"I've got a man looking for her right now," Armstrong admitted.

"Then, how about the guy in the sharp suit he was talking to just before that happened? I got the impression he wasn't exactly an upright citizen."

"Would your brother get involved with someone like that?" the sheriff asked.

"If he thought he could make a quick buck, I don't doubt it for a second." Alex felt somehow disloyal speaking that way about his last living kin, but what choice did he have?

"Any chance you caught his name?"

"I think my brother said it was Jackson."

"First or last name?"

Alex shook his head. "That's all I got. Sorry I can't help you."

Armstrong nodded. "I'll take a look myself. Is there anything else you want to add?"

Alex remembered the torn paper in his pocket. "Mor and I found this behind a dead receptacle in the room where Tony was killed." He handed it the sheriff, who took it and then studied it for a few moments.

Armstrong shook his head. "There's no reason to think this was related to his murder," he said as he handed it back to Alex.

"Not even from where it was found?"

"It sounds like it was hidden pretty carefully by someone. Alex, that doesn't jibe with the knife someone used on your brother. It was a murder of opportunity, and maybe even passion. This is just a dead end, trust me."

Alex was about to argue with the sheriff when Elise came hurrying up to them. "Alex, we need to talk."

The sheriff smiled slightly, but he was careful not to let Elise see it. "That's never good coming from a woman, is it?" he asked softly.

Alex was in no mood for the sheriff's humor. "Are we finished here?"

"For now. I'm sorry, but I've taken over the Main Keepers' Quarters. It shouldn't be more for than a day or two."

"Take your time. We don't have any guests scheduled for four days," Alex admitted.

"Why's that?"

"We were going to be on our honeymoon," Alex said simply.

The sheriff looked embarrassed about his lapse. "Sorry. That's right. I'll be in touch."

He tipped his hat to Elise, who had stood a little back so they could finish their conversation.

Elise hurried to Alex and said, "I don't know what to say. My father had no right—."

Alex cut her off, "To try to protect his daughter? He had every right. Elise, I don't blame him for telling the sheriff what he saw."

"You're kidding, right? I'm furious with him myself."

"If your dad hadn't told the sheriff about what happened, I was going to do it myself. We both know from experience that there can't be any secrets when it comes to a murder investigation."

"He still shouldn't have just volunteered it like that," Elise said.

"If you were my daughter, I would have done the exact same thing."

"I'm still making him apologize," Elise said.

"I'd really rather you didn't," Alex said.

"Too late," Elise said as her father walked toward them. He started to speak, but Alex beat him to it. "Sir, I appreciate you telling the sheriff what you saw last night. If you hadn't, I would have done it myself. For what it's worth, I didn't kill my brother, but you were well within your rights to say what you did to the sheriff."

Mr. Danton looked taken aback by Alex's statement. "Elise seems to feel otherwise."

"You did what you thought was right by her, even though it couldn't have been easy for you," Alex said. "I respect that."

Something seemed to dawn on the man's face. A few moments later, he said, "And I respect your attitude. I must admit I had my doubts about Elise marrying her boss, but you've set them all to rest. Welcome to the family. I'd be honored to give my daughter away to you tonight."

"I'm afraid that's not going to happen," Alex said. He turned to Elise and added, "Didn't you tell them?"

"I didn't have time," she admitted. "Dad, the wedding's off."

"For good?" the man asked.

"No, just until we find Tony's killer," Elise said.

"You know I don't like you meddling in murder," Mr. Danton said.

"Respectfully, I'm a grown woman. This involves Alex, and that means it involves me." She tried to smile as she added, "Clearly our honeymoon is off as well. Alex and I would love it if you and Mom would take our trip instead."

"That's out of the question," Mr. Danton said.

"I'm really sorry you feel that way. I hate the thought of just throwing that money away. We worked too hard to just let it go to waste," Alex said.

"I just wouldn't feel right benefiting from your misfortune," the man said.

"You'd be doing us a favor," Alex countered. "You're an innkeeper too, so surely you must understand. We all work hard for our money, and when we get the opportunity, we should get some joy out of it, don't you agree?"

"I don't know," he said, though it was clear he was torn.

Alex tried his best to smile. "I know it's an imposition, but it would mean a lot to me, to us, if you'd help us out here."

"Fine, we'll accept your generous offer," he said. "I'll go clear it with Mrs. Danton."

After he left, Elise asked, "How did you manage to do that? I wouldn't have been able to do that in a million years."

"We're not that different, you know."

"Us?" Elise asked as she touched his chest.

"Us," Alex said as he pointed to her father, and then to himself.

"You're different enough," Elise answered.

"We are both innkeepers, and we both love you. Do you need anything else?"

"No, that's enough for me," Elise said. "I suppose we should get the word out that the wedding has been canceled."

"Postponed, you mean," Alex corrected.

"Absolutely. We've got cake, food, people coming, and permission to turn on the lighthouse light. It's a shame to let it all go to waste."

"We can give the cake and the food to the family shelter," Alex said, "and folks will understand. One thing, though. If it's okay with you, I'd like to go ahead and light the light when it gets dark enough. For Tony."

"Of course," Elise said. "I'd better get inside. I have some telephone calls to make."

"I've got a better idea. Let's tell Emma, and she can handle it for us. Then we can go to Bear Rocks while there's still light, and try to forget for a few minutes that this ever happened."

"I like it," Elise said. "Meet you back here in three minutes."

Elise was as good as her word, and until the sun went down and it grew too cold, Alex and Elise spent the rest of the afternoon talking about everything in the world except their postponed wedding and Tony's murder.

Chapter 6

It was only when they were walking back to the Dual Keepers' Quarters that Elise brought it up. She stopped and took Alex's hands in hers. "It's almost time to light the beacon, but before we do, I want you to promise me something."

"Anything," Alex said.

"We're going to solve Tony's murder, and we're going to do it together. I wasn't his biggest fan, but whoever did this stole the most important day in my life from me, and even if it weren't your brother who was murdered, that makes it personal."

Alex chewed it over in his mind, as he'd been doing all afternoon despite his attempts to forget it, and he'd come to the same conclusion that they'd have to solve this crime themselves. "I promise."

"Good. I can't wait to marry you. I know it might be old fashioned, but I want to be Mrs. Alex Winston, and no murderer is going to stop that."

"I can't tell you how happy I am to hear you say that."

"What are you two talking about?" Emma asked as she approached them, hand in hand with her husband.

"How much we want to be married," Alex said.

Mor nodded. "Don't worry, you will be. And when all of this is over, we get to do everything again."

Emma looked sternly at her husband, and with a new bit of happiness in his voice, he said, "And when this is all over, we get to everything again." After he said it, he looked at his wife for her approval.

"That's better, Mor." She kissed him, and it was one of the few times that Mor looked smaller than he usually was.

To take the focus off of him, Mor looked at Alex and said, "We're solving this thing, right?"

"It's not going to be easy," Alex said. "Our two suspects

aren't staying at the inn. I'm not even certain that they're still in Elkton Falls."

"They're somewhere though, and wherever that is, we'll find them," Elise said. Alex loved hearing the determination in her voice.

"What's our first step?" Emma asked.

"We light the beacon, for Tony," Alex said simply as the last of the daylight faded.

They all nodded, and set about lighting Hatteras West to mark the passing of a Winston.

Alex offered to stand by the switch, but Emma offered instead. "You should go outside and look at it," she said. "You can't see it all from here, and if you're on the observation deck upstairs, it doesn't look like much, does it?"

"Thank you," Alex said, and hugged Emma. He sometimes forgot how strong she was under her extra weight, but Emma was solid muscle.

"You're welcome."

"Coming?" Alex asked Mor.

"If it's all the same to you, I think I'll stay right here."

Emma didn't protest, so Alex and Elise walked out into the night. They went back to Bear Rocks, and from their vantage point there, they could see the light shining out into the valley and hills that surrounded them. It never failed to take Alex's breath away, seeing the lighthouse lit. To her credit, Elise didn't say a word as they watched in silence. Her hand tightened around his, though, and he felt great comfort from her presence.

As soon as the allotted time was up, the light flicked out of existence.

"We should have brought a flashlight with us," Elise said.

"We don't need one. I grew up on these rocks, remember, and there's not a soul that knows them better than I do. They'd released their hands for a moment, but Alex reached again for Elise's, and gently guided her back to the path that led to the inn.

Mor and Emma were waiting for them at the base of the

lighthouse. The four of them stood there in silence, as though they were afraid to break the mood that seemed to surround them all. It was as though the lighthouse beam had muted even the night sounds around them.

Mor finally said, "Well, if we're going to get an early start on our hunt, we'd better call it a night."

He shook Alex's hand, waved to Elise, and then started to walk to his truck.

"Should we stay here with you tonight?" Emma asked. "You might need to have friends around you at a time like this."

"No, we'll be fine," Elise said. She hugged her friend, and then Emma joined her husband. Elise's parents were on the road headed for Williamsburg, and the other family and friends who'd come for the celebration had left as well. It appeared that no one wanted to linger at the inn, and Alex was glad for it. This was a time of mourning, not just for his brother, but for the loss, at least for today, of the wedding he'd so desperately hoped to have.

He and Elise walked inside, and Alex offered, "Should I light a fire to take the chill off?"

She shook her head. "Not tonight. If you don't mind, I think I'll turn in a little early."

He was disappointed to hear it, but he tried not to show it. "I understand."

She turned to him and asked, "Do you, Alex?"

"I get it, Elise. You're as sad as I am," Alex said.

"I wanted with all my heart to be Mrs. Winston by now," she said.

He wrapped her up in his arms. "It's just a delay, Elise."

She looked up at him. "Do you promise me that, Alex?"

"With every fiber of my being," he said. "Nothing else matters right now than finding Tony's killer. The second we do, I'm proposing to you again."

Elise smiled up at him. "Not necessary. You have a standing yes anytime you want to cash it in." She kissed him, and then pulled away. "I don't know how you do it, Alex, but you always seem to know how to make me feel better."

"What can I say? You bring it out in me, too."

"Good night, my love," she said.

He smiled at her. "Good night. I do love you."

Elise nodded gently. "I'm depending on it."

After she was in her room, Alex wondered if he should turn in himself. This day had turned into an awful mockery of what they'd had planned, and he remembered one of his favorite sayings. 'Man plans, God laughs.' It was never more true than it was right now.

Alex would have been pleased the next morning if he'd woken up to rain, sleet, snow, or even hail. It would have done much better to match his mood than the bright sunshine peeking in through his window. What right did the world have being happy on a day he should have been on his honeymoon? He got ready quickly, and walked out front, wondering what he needed to do to go in search of the suspects he'd met yesterday. They had to have a plan, but so far, Alex was stumped. Even the sheriff wasn't at all certain he'd be able to track down the man and woman from the rehearsal dinner. What chance would the four of them have?

Alex was still wondering about it when there was a knock at the front door. It was too early for Mor and Emma, and Alex wondered who it might be. If it was a wandering tourist looking for a place to stay, Alex was going to have to disappoint him.

To his shock, it was the man Tony had gotten into an argument at the dinner. It was all Alex could do not to cry out. "May I help you?"

The man nodded. "I need a room, and I was wondering if you could help me."

"I'd be delighted. How many nights will you be with us?"

"As long as it takes," the man muttered under his breath. Alex heard it, anyway.

"As long as what takes?" he asked.

"What? Never mind, I was just talking to myself." He reached into his pocket and pulled out a roll of bills. "Will this do for now?"

Alex nodded as took the cash. He would have offered the man a free room if it meant getting him to stay at the inn. At least one of their suspects was going to be right under their noses.

"Here's the register. You need to sign in."

The man didn't look all that pleased about it, but he took the pen and wrote something in the book Elise liked keeping up front. She thought it gave the place a certain amount of charm, and Alex had to agree with her.

Alex studied the quickly scrawled handwriting to confirm what he'd heard the night before, and then said, "Welcome to Hatteras West, Mr. Jackson."

"Sorry about your brother," he said as he looked around the lobby. "Do I have to stay in this building, or can I bunk over there?" he asked as he pointed to the Main Keeper's Quarters.

"Sorry, it's not available."

Jackson just shrugged at the news, as though he'd been expecting it.

"May I help you with your luggage?" Alex asked, a clear shot since the man wasn't carrying so much as a notebook.

"Don't worry about me. I'll get it later." He reached for the key Alex was holding out to him.

"I'd be glad to show you your room," Alex said.

Jackson frowned, and then said, "I'll see it later. For now, I'd like to walk around some."

"Fine. If you need me, just ring the bell."

Mr. Jackson reached down and pushed the bell once, then went out the door.

Alex debated waking Elise to tell him the news, when he was surprised to see her coming down the stairs along.

"I didn't even realize you were up," he said.

"I've been up for an hour. I didn't want to wake you. I was just seeing about our guest."

"He just left," Alex said. "How did you know about that?"

"It could be because our 'he' is really a 'she'."

Alex was confused now. "There's no way that was a woman who just walked out of here."

"I'm talking about Monique Combs. I just checked her in and got her settled in the Carolina Jasmine suite."

Alex bit his lower lip. "I didn't think we were taking on new guests."

Elise looked excited as she said, "She's the woman from the rehearsal dinner, the one who slapped Tony."

Alex didn't like that a bit. "And I just checked in the man he had an argument with."

"It's a little too much to take as coincidence, isn't it?" Elise asked.

Alex nodded. "Don't kid yourself. They're here looking for something, and I can't help but wonder if it's that little piece of paper that Mor and I found in the Main Keepers' Quarters."

"I looked at it, too, and it looked like nothing special to me."

Alex just shrugged. "Then maybe there's something else they're after, but at least we won't have to go hunting for them now. They came to us."

Elise nodded. "It's handy that we can grill them right here."

"Only they shouldn't know they're being questioned," Alex added.

"This isn't my first time investigating a murder, remember?"

He laughed at that. "Don't remind me. How many times have we come close to getting caught snooping by one of our guests?"

"I try to forget things like that," she said with a grin, "but the answer is too many, I can tell you that." She looked around to make sure no one was nearby, and asked softly, "Should we search Jackson's room for clues?"

"That would be kind of pointless, since he hasn't even been there yet. He got the key, and then decided that he wanted to take a walk."

"You don't think he's out strolling around though, do you?" Elise asked.

"No," Alex admitted. "I wanted to give him time to go over to the other building before I surprised him."

"Let's go, then," Elise said.

Alex shook his head. "It might be dangerous. You should stay here. Call Sheriff Armstrong if something happens to me."

Elise shook her head resolutely. "You're not going anywhere without me, mister. If one of us goes, the other tags along. I'm not about to lose my groom before we've had a chance to say our vows."

"Then technically, I wouldn't be your groom yet, would I?"

Elise didn't respond, just headed for the front door. "Do you want to stand here and have a debate, or should we start snooping?"

"I vote for snooping," Alex said.

"That's the man I want to marry," she said, and the two of them left the Dual and headed for the Main.

Alex tried the main door, and found that it was still locked.

"It doesn't mean he didn't find another way inside," Elise suggested.

"There's only one way to find out."

They used his key to open the main door, now that the police tape was gone. The sheriff must have moved quickly to search the building, and Alex wondered if perhaps the search had been done too hastily. There was a great deal of space there, and he believed that it was possible that he and his force had missed something. If they had, he was sure that he and Elise would find it. After all, no one knew the inn as well as they did.

After a quick inventory of the rooms, Alex said, "It's pretty clear that he's not here. Should we go looking for him outside, or look around a little more carefully while we're here?"

"I vote we inspect the building before anyone else can get in," Elise said.

"That's not a bad idea," Alex answered.

"Why, because you like agreeing with me?" she asked with a smile.

"It doesn't hurt, does it? Besides, that's as good an idea as any."

"Then let's start our treasure hunt. What exactly are we looking for?"

"Anything that doesn't fit," Alex said. "And we should start in the room where Mor and I found Tony." Alex hated the thought of going back in there, but he really didn't have any choice. Sooner or later he'd have to face the memory of seeing his brother in the bathtub, and the quicker he could put that image behind him, the better.

They pulled the mattress off the bed, looked behind the lighthouse painting on the wall, even checked under the bed.

Elise frowned at Alex. "Nothing's out of order," she said. "The floor needs a good waxing, doesn't it?"

"And the drapes need to be replaced too."

She looked at him quizzically, and he explained, "I had some time on my hands waiting for the sheriff to take my call."

"What should we do?"

"We have to keep looking, no matter how painful it might be," Alex said. He couldn't believe that Tony could be killed so easily without at least one clue being left behind. He'd tried to put it off, but he finally forced himself to walk into the bathroom.

Elise touched his hand, and then took it in hers as they went inside. Alex felt a rush from her touch, and a new determination to push his way through this.

He looked around the bathroom, trying to take everything

in. It was odd what the police had confiscated. Two towels were gone, he still couldn't find that blasted mat, the shower curtain was missing now along with a complimentary bottle of shampoo, but the packet with a shower cap and razor was still there, along with an unwrapped bar of soap in the shower, an unopened bar of soap by the sink, and a wrapped roll of toilet paper on the back of the toilet. Elsewhere on the sink, he did a quick inventory of the mouthwash, hand towels, facial tissues; still there, but all out of their regular order. The towels had clearly been unfolded, and then folded back up, but nothing else looked as though it had been touched. Still, nothing stood out as he purposely kept his glance away from the tub as much as he could.

"There's not a thing wrong here that I can see that a little tidying up wouldn't take care of," Elise said, though it was clear that she was much more focused on Alex than she was on exploring the room. "Come on," she said as she tugged at his hand. "They didn't miss anything." Alex let himself be led out of the bathroom, but something stuck in his mind, something he'd seen, but failed to recognize the significance of.

"Hang on a second."

"Alex, don't put yourself through this."

"Something doesn't add up."

Elise followed him back into the bathroom, and as Alex double-checked what he'd seen, Elise followed his gaze, listening as he explained what had bothered him. "That soap in the dish in the shower has been unwrapped, but the one at the sink hasn't been touched. That doesn't make any sense. If Tony or anyone else in here had washed his hands, he would have used the soap at the sink, but it hasn't even been opened. Why put an opened bar in the stall if he used it to wash his hands? He wasn't exactly over here so he could take a shower."

Elise frowned. "You're right, Alex. It doesn't make sense."

Alex reached for the soap, and as soon as he touched it,

he knew that it had been run under hot water at some time recently from the tackiness of its surface. It felt oddly heavy as well, and when Alex turned it over, he saw why.

Sunk slightly into the back of the bar of soap was a gold coin, something that looked quite valuable, and ancient as well, with markings and engravings like he'd never seen before.

Alex had to wonder if that was what the killer had been looking for. One old gold coin didn't seem to be enough of a motive for murder, but a handful of them might. "Let's look around again, but this time, we need to be creative. Search for anything that might hide more gold coins, no matter how strange a hiding place it might seem."

It wasn't until Alex got to the box of tissues in the bedroom that they found anything else. The box weighed considerably more than it should have, and it was clear that Armstrong and his men hadn't done that thorough a search of the place after all.

Alex tore open the tissue box, pulling out nearly a full batch of the white sheets until he unveiled what was hidden beneath them.

Inside, there were twenty-nine coins identical to the one Alex had found in the soap.

They weren't exactly thirty pieces of silver, but Alex had to wonder if they had led to betrayal anyway.

Chapter 7

"What should we do?" Elise asked. "Do we need to call the sheriff?"

"Not yet," Alex answered, careful not to touch any of the coins just in case there were fingerprints on any of them. "After all, we're already not telling him about two suspects staying here with us at the inn. If we hand all of this over to him at once, what chance is there that we solve Tony's murder ourselves?"

"I suppose so," Elise said. "But when he finds out, he's not going to like it."

"And that would be different from how he normally feels about me exactly how?" Alex asked as he got to work. Removing the shower cap from its paper sleeve, Alex carefully dumped the coins in it. The cap nearly broke under the pressure of the weight, but Alex held them carefully and tied off the opening. After he did that, he wrapped the soap, along with its coin, in a hand towel, and then carefully put it all into the clean liner of the trashcan in the bedroom.

"Aren't we withholding evidence if we don't tell him about what we've found?" Elise asked.

"I'd say that's true, but Armstrong's already searched this room. If there's a way we can keep our discovery secret for a day or two, we might be able to work it to our advantage."

"How are we going to do that?"

Alex shrugged. "I'm still thinking about that. I don't have a plan yet, but I have high hopes. After all, I'm doubly motivated to wrap this up as quickly as I can." He looked carefully at her. "Are you okay with that?"

"Maybe we'll get jail cells that touch," she said, trying to force a light grin. "At least we could hold hands then."

"I'll see if I can pull some strings if it comes up," Alex replied. As he looked at what they'd found, he added, "I can't imagine what Tony was doing with these coins."

"Are they real gold?" Elise asked.

Alex hefted the weight again. "If they aren't, the weight is matched pretty closely. What was Tony doing with these?"

"Any thoughts?"

"I have a hunch they were part of some kind of scam," Alex said. "I hate to speak ill of the dead, but it's not going to help us find Tony's killer if we don't accept the fact that my brother was a bit of a lowlife."

"He fell on some hard times, that's all," Elise said.

Alex knew that she was just trying to help, but it wouldn't work. He knew his brother for what the man had really become. If he accepted that, even used his knowledge of Tony to his advantage, it might just help him find his brother's killer.

"There you are. We thought you might have bugged out on us already," Mor said as Alex and Elise walked back into the lobby of the Dual Keepers' Quarters. They'd done their best to straighten the room back up before they'd left, even taking fresh soap and tissues from the maid's closet down the hall. When they left the scene of the crime, it was as much like it had been when they'd first searched it as they could manage. Alex had closed a paperclip in the lower part of the door so that if it were opened, he'd see it on the floor. It wouldn't keep anyone out, but it should tell him if someone had broken in.

Alex shook his head. "No, but things have changed. We're not going in search of our suspects."

"Why not?" Emma asked. "I thought you wanted to solve your brother's murder."

"I do, but we got lucky. Our suspects found us instead."

Mor whistled softly. "Are you telling me that they had the nerve to come back here, after what happened? They have to know that they'll be suspects in Tony's murder. It had to be something pretty compelling to get them here."

Alex looked around just to be sure they were alone. He

still wasn't satisfied, though. "Let's go into my office for a second."

Mor and Emma looked puzzled by the request, but they followed it nonetheless.

Once the door was safely closed behind them, Alex unwrapped the bar of soap housing the first coin he'd found and handed it to Mor. "Be careful. There may be fingerprints."

"Gotcha," Mor said. He studied the coin, still encased in the soap, and then handed it to Emma as he said, "I'm guessing you found this in the room were Tony was murdered."

"We did," Elise replied.

"Is it real?" Mor asked.

Emma said, "Unless I miss my guess, it appears to be off the Santa Angela shipwreck. Most folks believe it was lost off the Florida Keys, but no one's been able to find it."

"Until now," Mor said.

Alex knew that Emma was an amateur gemologist and generalized treasure hunter. Until he learned otherwise, he was going to go with her theory. "So, do you think it's legitimate?"

"I can't say for sure without running some tests. It would help if I could study the back of it so I could get a closer look at what's there."

"Hang on a second," Alex said as he had a sudden thought. "Mor, how are you at counterfeiting?"

Mor got it instantly, a quickness that Alex cherished about his friend. "How close does it have to be to pass as legit?"

"As close as you can manage," Alex said.

Mor thought about it, and then after a few moments, he said, "I'll need the real coin for the casting. I think lead will do nicely, with some gold paint to make it look real. Sorry if I mess up the fingerprints on it, but there's really no way around it."

"You can use it," Elise said. "It's got to be clean."

"I'd hope so," Mor said.

"Of fingerprints," she added.

"Alex?" Mor asked.

"Go ahead."

Mor took out his pocketknife, selected a blade, and then pried the coin of the soap. "This will do just fine," he said as he hoisted the coin in his hand.

Emma reached out. "Let me see that."

He did as he was told, and after a moment, Emma said, "Don't hold me to it, but I'm guessing this is the real thing. How on earth did your brother get his hands on it?"

"I wish I could ask him," Alex said.

"I'm sorry, Alex," Emma said. "I didn't mean anything by it."

"Hang on. There's more," Alex said as he pulled out the shower-cap bag and dumped the rest of the coins out onto the washcloth sitting on the desk.

Mor whistled softly. "My, oh my."

"Don't get too excited. I have a hunch these aren't real. Emma, what do you think?"

"Let me look," Emma said. She glanced around Alex's office, found a cellophane wrapped plastic cup, and removed it from its sleeve.

Putting her hand into the plastic, Emma chose a coin from the washcloth cache, held it for a moment, barely glanced at it, and then put it back in the pile, her expression ever cryptic. She chose three more coins at random, barely glancing at them as she did so, and then said, "They're all fakes. How did you know?"

"I'm betting my brother tried double-crossing the wrong person," Alex said. "Who knows where the real coin came from, but he must have had the counterfeits made up off them. I wonder how many copies he sold before he finally got caught?"

Elise touched his shoulder. "Alex, I'm so sorry."

"I just wish I could say that I was surprised," Alex said. "Mor, how long to make the dummies?"

"Alex, I don't mind doing it, but why not just use these?"

"We might need them as evidence," Alex said. "I'd feel better if we used coins we make ourselves for bait."

"Understood. If I bust my hump, I can have them ready in about three hours."

"It's that easy?" Elise asked.

"I didn't say that, but I've done it before, not with coins, mind you, but the process is the same. I'm going to do sand castings. They're quick and dirty, and I can use my tools to polish them right up. Piece of cake."

Alex glanced at his watch. "If you don't mind, I'd appreciate it if you'd get right on it."

"How about me?" Emma asked. "Do I have a task as well?"

Alex knew that Emma was a whiz at researching things on the Internet. "Dig into this coin's history, and the shipwreck you think it came off of. Find out what the rumors are, if anyone's claimed to have found it in the past." He nearly didn't add the last bit on his mind, but there was no way he could let that particular stone go unturned. "Do a search on my brother, too. See what you can turn up."

"Even if it's bad news?" Emma asked. It was clear the large woman was uncomfortable with the prospect of digging up even more dirt on his brother.

"Make it as thorough as you can," Alex said. "We need to know what he's been up to lately."

"Got it," Emma said.

"We meet back up here this afternoon, then," Alex said.

"What are you two going to be doing in the meantime?" Mor asked.

"Two things," Alex answered. "First, we're going to see what we can uncover about our guests, and second, we need to come up with a plan on how best to use those coins you'll be making for us."

Alex opened the door and followed his friends outside.

"See you soon," he said.

They waved as they got into their car and drove away.

"Where should we begin?" Elise asked.

"We need to put those counterfeit coins away in our safe," Alex said. "Real or not, they might be the evidence we need to find Tony's killer."

Their female guest came down the steps just after Emma and Mor left the inn. Alex approached her and said, "I'm sorry, but I don't believe we've met. My name is Alex Winston." He held out his hand, and she took it hesitantly. Alex felt a band-aid on her hand in his grip, and he wondered if that was why she hadn't been eager to shake hands, or if it was because she'd been the one who had killed his brother. Alex watched her face, searching for some kind of reaction, but he didn't see anything in her eyes to betray the fact that she'd known his brother. She let go of his hand and took a step back from him.

"I'm Monique Combs," she said simply.

"It's nice to meet you," Alex said. "What brings you to our inn?"

Monique clearly didn't care to answer that. "Nothing more than a whim," she said. "If it's all the same to you, I thought I'd take a stroll around the grounds."

She tried to brush past them, but Alex took a step and placed himself between her and the door. "How well did you know my brother?"

"Your brother?"

Alex wasn't buying the innocent routine. Normally he was quite careful with his guests, but this woman wasn't here to take in the ambiance of the lighthouse or the inn. "Tony Winston. He's the man you slapped at my rehearsal dinner two nights ago. Funny, but I didn't remember inviting you to the event."

"That's because you didn't," Monique said a little petulantly. "Tony did."

Whether that was true or not, there was really no way of proving it, since Alex couldn't exactly ask his brother to confirm it.

Elise said, "You had an odd way of thanking him for the invitation. Everyone at our party saw you slap him."

Alex added, "You looked mad enough to kill him."

She laughed off the accusation. "Okay, if you want to talk about it, we'll talk about it. Tony and I had a great many highs and lows in our relationship. It was nothing for us to argue one minute and fall into bed together the next."

"You don't seem all that torn up by his murder," Alex said, a touch of anger leaking through into his voice.

"We all mourn in different ways, don't we? Tony told me often about this place, growing up here with you. I won't be in Elkton Falls ever again, so I wanted to experience a little of what he told me about firsthand."

Alex didn't believe her, and everything she said from that point on would be carefully tested and weighed. Tony had hated the lighthouse and the inn growing up. He hadn't been able to wait to get away, and there was no way Alex would ever believe his brother would look back on his childhood with anything even approaching nostalgia.

"How did you two meet?" Elise asked.

"It's really not something I care to discuss," she said. "Now if you'll excuse me, I really do need some air."

Monique swept out of there, and Elise looked at Alex. "I'm sorry. I didn't mean to drive her off."

"Don't blame yourself. She couldn't wait to get out of here," Alex said. "I wouldn't believe the lighthouse was outside our door if she told me. I'd have to go out and check it myself."

"What do you think she's lying about, Tony, their relationship, or what?"

"Everything," Alex said. "My brother hated it here. There's no way he'd ever speak fondly of it. Of that I'm certain."

"Could he have changed in the years since he was away from it?" Elise asked.

Alex loved her for the thought, and that she was always looking for the silver lining to any cloud. "No. It took everything I could do to get him here for our wedding, and if he hadn't thought of scamming me out of money, I doubt he would have come back even for that."

Elise took his words on faith. "Then we need to uncover her real story."

Alex nodded. "There's only one way to do that. It's time to violate her privacy. You don't have to come with me, if you're not comfortable with that."

"She lied to us. As far as I'm concerned, she forfeited any rights she had. Besides," she added with a smile, "we're innkeepers. It's our duty to make sure our guests are well taken care of. I believe Monique needs more towels than I put in her room earlier."

"Then we really should remedy that," Alex said, matching her smile.

They started for her room upstairs, and Elise paused at the linen closet. As she grabbed more towels, she said, "Just in case she comes back."

"I believe we'll have a harder time explaining why it took two innkeepers to deliver them."

Elise shrugged. "I'll tell her you were supervising me."

He kissed her, and then asked, "Is that what we're calling it now?"

"Work now, play later," Elise said.

The two of them stepped inside, and were immediately taken aback. Monique had been in the room less than two hours, but it looked as though a hurricane had hit it. Clothes were scattered everywhere, the quilt Alex's mother had made was haphazardly thrown on the floor, and the faucet in the bathroom had been left on, leaving a stream of water running down the drain.

Alex immediately shut it off. "She's quite the whirlwind, isn't she?"

"More like a slob," Elise said. "How can anyone live like this?" She started to straighten up, but Alex took her hand.

"We're not here to clean up," he said. "Look for clues."

"Anything in particular?" she asked.

"Just something that doesn't match what we know so far."

Elise nodded, and as she began to search, Alex helped.

He found a large black handbag tucked under one pillow, and as he pulled it out, he handed it to Elise. "Look at this."

"You can search it yourself," she said.

Alex looked at the bag as though it were radioactive. "I learned long ago that there were some things that a man shouldn't do, and near the top of the list is going into a woman's purse."

"Not even his girlfriend's, or his wife's?" Elise asked as she started to open the bag. ˙

"Especially not then," Alex answered.

Elise smiled briefly, then began hunting through the bag. Alex wanted to stay and watch, but he wasn't at all certain how much time they had, so he began looking in the drawers, and then the bathroom. If Elise found anything, he knew that she'd tell him about it. He wasn't having much luck when he spotted something in the garbage can in the bathroom. In the bottom of the can, hidden by some old newspapers, Alex found a slim catalogue with listings in it.

It was from an auction house, and several items had been circled on the pages as he glanced through it.

Including a single rare coin from the 1600s.

"Elise, look at this," he said as he walked into the bedroom.

She didn't even look up.

Alex approached her quickly. "What is it? What's wrong?"

A great many things were spread out on the bed, from a compact to lipstick to a small brush. Along with those items, there were three pens, a battered old day planner, and a cancelled ticket from a movie theater in Charlotte.

"Look," Elise said as she held the bag out toward Alex. With a slight hesitation, he leaned over and looked down. There, in the bottom of the bag, were two things that alarmed him more than he could imagine; a small lady's handgun with a pearl handle, and his brother's class ring from college.

"Tony never took this off," Alex said as he reached for the ring. "It was his pride and joy."

"Well, she got it somehow. That's not what's worrying me, though. She has a gun, Alex."

Alex shrugged. "Tony was stabbed with a knife, remember?"

Elise nodded, and then said, "I know that, but wouldn't you say this tells us the girl has a predisposition for violence?"

"Who knows why she carries it? A lot of people have guns. Just because we don't doesn't mean anything." Alex gingerly picked up the weapon, opened the breach, and removed all of its bullets.

"What are you doing? She's bound to notice that her ammunition is missing."

"Maybe so, but I feel better knowing that her claws have been pulled."

Elise stared at it, and then said, "We could just take the gun ourselves."

"I'll confiscate her bullets, but I won't steal her gun," Alex said.

"That's an awfully fine line."

"I agree, but it's as far as I'm willing to go."

Elise frowned. "What if she has more ammo?"

"Then we're in trouble, because that means I've misjudged her. I can see Monique carrying this with her for protection, but from everything we've seen, can you imagine that she had the forethought to plan anything as rational as packing extra ammunition? If she'd brought a gun with her to kill Tony, I have a feeling she would have used it. It wouldn't surprise me at all if we find out Jackson's got a weapon himself, along with who knows what else in his arsenal?"

"I don't disagree with that, but if we're wrong, the learning curve is going to be kind of steep."

"We could always hide it under the bed," Alex suggested.

"How could that make any sense?" Elise asked.

"If she asks us about it, we can say we were making the bed and her purse fell off it. The gun could have gotten accidentally kicked under the bed and out of sight."

Elise shook her head. "That's an awfully big line of coincidences, don't you think?"

"It's not all that important that she believe us," Alex said. "What matters is that it might be true, and the shadow of that doubt is all we really need."

"We can't do that," Elise said. "I don't see how she could believe it for a second."

"Then we'll have to be happy doing this." Alex pocketed the bullets, and then started to reach for Tony's ring.

Elise noticed him hesitate. "Go ahead and take it. It's rightfully yours."

"Not if Tony really gave it to Monique. It's not mine, legally or morally."

"Alex, did your brother even have a will?" Elise asked.

"I have no idea how current it might be. Uncle Jase wrote wills for both of us when our folks died, but mine's changed since then, and I can't imagine that his hasn't as well."

"Really?"

He nodded. "Six months after we met, I made you my sole beneficiary. If something happens to me, Hatteras West is all yours."

Elise took the news like a blow to the chest, reeling back a step before catching herself. When Alex looked at her, it appeared that she was crying.

"I'm sorry," he said quickly. "I didn't mean to saddle you with this place. It's just that it was clear that you loved Hatteras West just as much as I do. I thought of Emma and Mor, but they aren't suited to be innkeepers, and besides, I'm leaving all of my books, my tools, and a nice piece of change for Mor. But you get everything else."

She was openly sobbing now. Alex put his arms around her, and then said, "I don't know what to do."

"Just hold me," she said, and he did as he was asked, taking in the smell of her hair, the way she felt in his arms.

After a few moments, she pulled away. He said lamely, "I really am sorry. I thought it was a good idea at the time."

"Trust me, it does. It means more to me than your marriage proposal," Elise said simply.

"I'm not sure how to take that, to be honest with you," Alex said.

Elise just laughed. "Alex, I knew in my heart that you loved me, but to entrust Hatteras West to me says it more than a thousand poems and a million boxes of chocolate." She kissed him, long and soundly, and then said, "I love you, too."

"That's good," Alex said. "For a second, I thought I might have blown it."

"My dear Alex, I'm not sure you could if you tried, but do us both a favor."

"What's that?"

"Don't try," she said with a smile. "Now, back to your brother."

"I'm not sure Tony had anything to bequeath, so it may be a moot point."

"Is there any way to find out?" Elise asked.

"I'm not sure. Why, do you think it's important?"

"It could be," she said. "Who stands to be better off with Tony dead?"

"Hello?" they both heard a familiar voice call out from downstairs. "Is anybody here?"

It was the sheriff, and knowing him, he wasn't there to compliment them on their new drapes.

Chapter 8

Elise started jamming everything back into Monique's purse as she said, "Go talk to him. I'll be down in a minute."

Alex did as she asked, and he found Sheriff Armstrong standing there with his hand on the front door.

"Here I am," Alex said.

"I was about to give up on you."

"Rooms need to be cleaned and chores have to be done, no matter what else is going on around here," Alex said.

"Understood." The sheriff stared down at the hardwood floor, and then said, "I just got the report from the coroner's office. Your brother was killed between one and three am."

Alex realized that it had to have been Tony leaving the inn. That door slam had marked the beginning of the end for his brother. What if he'd gone out into the night looking for him? Would his brother still be alive, or would Alex have joined him in death?   As he considered the ramifications of what he hadn't done, Alex realized that the sheriff had asked him something, but he couldn't for the life of him remember what it had been.

"Excuse me?"

"Are you going to make me say it again?" the sheriff asked.

"I'm sorry, I zoned out there for a second."

The sheriff took in a deep breath of air, let it out, and then said, "I don't mean to be indelicate, but I have to ask you this question. Can anyone confirm where you were between one and three the night of the murder?"

"Elise can," Alex said.

The sheriff actually blushed slightly as he nodded. "I'll have to have her confirm it, there's no easy way around that, but it's good enough for me. Ordinarily it wouldn't be any of my business."

Alex couldn't believe the man. "We were sitting on the

couch the entire time drinking hot chocolate and reminiscing about our lives since Elise came to the inn."

"That was about the time that Reg Wellington was murdered, wasn't it?"

"Exactly that time," Alex replied, surprised that the sheriff had remembered Elise's first days at the inn. Then again, when it was tied so closely with a murder, it made perfect sense.

"She'll be able to confirm that?" Armstrong asked.

"Confirm what?" Elise asked as she came down the steps and joined them.

Alex started to explain when Armstrong held up a hand. "Alex, I need a minute with her. Go out on the porch. Now."

He was about to ask why when he realized that the sheriff was trying to confirm his alibi. Alex didn't want there to be any hint of suspicion, or impropriety, about what they'd been doing the night before, so he nodded and did as he was asked.

A minute later, the sheriff came out and rejoined him. "Where's Elise?" he asked.

"She had to answer a phone call."

"Did she back me up?"

"To the T," Armstrong said. "It was off just enough to be convincing."

"What parts didn't we agree on?" Alex asked.

"Doesn't matter. I believe you both, that's all that counts. It looks like you're in the clear."

"That's good to hear," Alex admitted. He'd been under the sheriff's scrutiny before when it came to murder, and he didn't like it one bit.

"Well, I won't trouble you anymore," the sheriff said.

Alex thought about telling him about their two guests, especially since they'd found the gun in Monique's purse, but something made him hold the information back. This was his brother's murder he was investigating, and he couldn't just hand it all over to someone else.

There was one thing he could ask, though. "Sheriff, I

need to know something, and I'm hoping you can tell me."

"Depends on what it is," the sheriff said. "I can't reveal much about an ongoing police investigation, so if it has something to do with the case, I can't tell you much."

"It's personal," Alex said. He had a ready excuse as to why he wanted the information, and only part of his rationalization was a lie. "Have you found Tony's will? We've never been close, but I'd always hoped that someday we could work things out. Finding out he thought of me, if only for a moment, when he was making out his will would make all of this a little easier to take."

Armstrong nodded. "It's perfectly understandable. From what I understand, he didn't have much, but what he did have is coming straight to you."

Alex wouldn't have guessed that answer with a thousand tries. "You're kidding."

"Nope, that's why I came out here hoping you had an alibi. If it does turn out that Tony was worth something, your reasons to be a suspect just doubled."

"I'm glad Elise and I had a craving for hot chocolate last night," Alex said.

"You can say that again. It probably kept you from going to jail today."

As the sheriff drove off, Elise joined Alex on the porch. "Did he believe us?" Elise asked.

"He didn't have much choice. You turned out to be a very good alibi."

"Glad to be of service," Elise said.

"Who was on the phone?"

"My folks. They wanted to thank us again for their vacation." She laughed a little.

"What's so funny?"

"We booked the honeymoon suite, remember? Dad can't get over the round bed, and it appears that Mom won't get out of the heart-shaped bathtub. They're thinking about putting a honeymoon suite in their inn back home."

Alex laughed, happy for the momentary break. "We're not making one here, though, are we?"

"No, I think we're good, at least for now," Elise said. "What should we do now?"

"I keep wondering where Mr. Jackson slipped off to. His car's in the lot, so he has to be on foot somewhere."

The wind blew a particular way, and Alex and Elise heard a man's voice say, "Why should I share any of it with you? The gold's all mine. I already paid for it."

Alex took Elise's hand, and the two of them left the porch to see who exactly was arguing over what they believed was real gold.

"The coins are mine," Monique said. "And I have no intention of sharing any of them once I find them." Alex and Elise heard her talking near the lighthouse, so they moved along the red brick base until they could hear better without being seen.

A man's voice that Alex recognized as Jackson's said, "I don't care if you killed him for them. It doesn't matter to me. I just want what's mine."

Monique sounded shocked as she replied, "I would never kill him. I loved that man. Besides, Tony promised them all to me as a wedding present."

"Why would he do that? You weren't even engaged," Jackson said.

"We were so."

"Then where's your ring?" he asked.

"It's in my purse. Tony couldn't afford the kind of engagement ring he wanted to give me just yet, so until he could make one last deal, he gave me his college class ring instead."

"Why would you keep it in your bag?" Jackson asked.

"What am I, in high school? Did you expect me to wear it on a chain around my neck like some silly schoolgirl?"

"I don't care where you wear it, the gold's mine. I don't care what he promised you. I already paid for it, and the crook cheated me."

Monique laughed without joy. "That's rich. You're calling Tony a crook? I know all about you. He told me about you and your employer, and how you've been putting the squeeze on him for months. He was getting out from under you, so you killed him, didn't you? It wouldn't be the first time you stabbed someone with a knife. Tony told me that was your style."

"How stupid do you think I am?" Jackson asked. "With him dead, there's no way we get our investment back."

"My employer," Jackson said. "That's why I'm here looking for the coins. He had to have stashed them somewhere around here."

"Well, I'm not going to help you look."

Jackson barked out his next words. "Do you think that crazy innkeeper's going to turn them over to either one of us when he finds them? He may be a hick, but I doubt that he's that big a moron. I'm betting if we keep standing around here debating it, nobody's going to make out but him."

Alex shook his head at the words of derision aimed at him, and Elise patted his arm. He wanted to protest, but he knew it would be exactly the wrong thing to do.

"If I find them first, I'm keeping them all for myself," Monique said.

"Good luck with that."

"Finding them, or keeping them?" Monique asked. Alex could hear a taste of fear in her voice. She truly was frightened by Jackson's presence, and he couldn't blame her. The man seemed ruthless, willing to stop at nothing to get what he thought belonged to him.

"Both," Jackson said.

"What if we worked together?" Monique asked, unable to keep the angst out of her voice. "How could I ever trust you?" she asked him, which Alex thought was a perfectly reasonable question.

"The same way I have to trust you, on faith," Jackson said. "We'll split what we find, right down the middle."

"I don't know," Monique said hesitantly.

"I don't have all day, lady. What's it going to be? Yes or no?"

"Yes," she said. "Do you have a plan?"

"I've been thinking about breaking into the other building again, but I don't want to get caught doing it this time. They nearly nailed me before. That's where you come in."

"I'm not some common thief," she said.

"I'm not asking you to do anything illegal. Just keep the innkeeper and his maid occupied while I dig around some. I had to slip out the back window when they came over there snooping around the last time."

"Do you think they found anything?" Monique asked.

"No, I doubt they even know what's going on."

"So, we're splitting the coins," she recounted. "And you're going back to your employer with less than you are supposed to have. How can I believe you're willing to settle for half of what you think is all rightfully yours?"

"Tony had more than coins," Jackson said.

"What are you talking about?"

"He stole something else from my employer that's more important than gold, and I mean to get it back."

There was more than a hint of avarice in Monique's voice as she asked, "What is it? Is it valuable?"

"Not to anyone but my boss. It's just a slip of paper."

Bingo. Alex and Mor had been right after all. The paper they'd found in the room where Tony had been murdered was tied into the case.

He just didn't know how yet.

"I'm taking off," Jackson said as he voice suddenly grew louder. "Just do your part and nobody has to get hurt."

"No one else, you mean," she said. "Tony's dead, isn't he?"

"Sure, if you're counting him."

Alex grabbed Elise's hand and pulled her away. There was no way they could get across the grass and back to the inn before Jackson and Monique spotted them.

"Are we going to do this right now?" Monique asked.

Alex looked wildly around. There was only one choice. They had to go up if they didn't want to be caught. Alex raced up the steps to the lighthouse, with Elise close behind him. As he opened the door, he could hear Jackson say faintly, "Not now. Tonight at nine, when no one else is around."

He closed the lighthouse door softly behind him, and then locked it.

It was a good thing he had. Ten seconds after he dead bolted it, the handle jiggled a little. "This stupid thing is locked," Jackson said from the other side of the door.

"What of it?" Monique answered him.

"What kind of lighthouse stays locked all day so the guests can't get in?"

"You can check it out later," Monique said. "We don't want to look suspicious."

"I could break into this door with a credit card in three seconds," Jackson said.

"Let's just go," she answered. "We don't want to make them suspicious."

Jackson's laugh was cold and full of scorn. Alex had no trouble believing that he was a cold blooded killer. "Neither one of them has a clue. The only we'll get caught is if we get sloppy, or they get lucky."

After the voices were gone, Alex hurried up the steps to the first window. As he looked out, he saw them going their separate ways. Jackson got into his car and drove off, while Monique walked into the inn.

"Let's go," Alex said.

Elise followed, and as they were hurrying back to the Dual Keepers' Quarters, she said, "We can't just walk in the front door now. She'll suspect we were eavesdropping."

"We can go in the back way, though."

They made it around the inn without being seen, and walked out into the lobby, where they found Monique at the desk, repeatedly ringing the bell there.

"Sorry, we were doing inventory in back," Alex said, trying his best to slow his breathing.

"We were counting towels," Elise said. "As a matter of fact, we left some extra in your room a little earlier today."

Monique was not at all pleased by that news. "You were in my room?"

"It's a part of the service we offer here," Alex said as smoothly as he could manage.

"I'm a very private person," Monique said. "I'd appreciate it if you didn't go in there again during my stay."

"What about to clean the place, swap out the towels, and change the sheets?" Elise asked.

"If I need anything, I'll let you know."

Alex nodded. "Whatever you'd like."

"Good. Now, is there any place to eat in town? No offense, but I need to get away from the inn for awhile. Too many memories, you know?"

"We have a nice place in Elkton Falls called Mamma Ravolini's," Alex said. "It's got all kinds of charm, and good food, too."

"Where exactly is it?" Monique asked.

Alex offered, "Drive into town. You can't miss it. Tell Irma we sent you."

"The woman's name is really Irma Ravolini?" Monique asked incredulously.

"No, it's Irma Bean. She thought Ravolini sounded more exotic when she first opened the place."

Monique merely shook her head. "Whatever."

Alex hated the expression, but he kept that fact to himself. If it were true that Tony had proposed to this vapid woman, he wouldn't have been surprised. She seemed to be his type, a little flash, and even less substance.

"If I don't go there, is there anywhere else to eat?"

"You could always go to Buck's Grill. They serve diner food, and their meatloaf is particularly good."

"Okay, I'm sure I can find something at one of those places."

She started to head upstairs, and Alex couldn't help asking, "I thought you were going out?"

"Not this early. I may take a nap, so don't disturb me."

"No, ma'am," he said.

After she was gone, Alex said, "She's checking on her gun right now."

"If you were dealing with Jackson, wouldn't you want to be armed? The real question is, is she looking for her ammunition, too? What if something happens to her because we stole her bullets and she couldn't defend herself?"

"Should I give them back? How is that going to work out?"

"Let's wait and see if she says anything about them being missing."

"I have a feeling if she discovers they are missing, we'll know about it in a minute," Alex said. He started straightening magazines in the lobby while Elise pretended to dust the furniture. After ten minutes, Monique didn't reappear, so they decided that they were safe. It had been a rash act stealing the bullets, and Alex knew it. Not only did it give away the fact that they'd been snooping in her purse, but it also showed they knew she was armed. He just hoped that he didn't live to regret the impulse. Even worse, if something happened to Monique, Alex wasn't sure that he'd ever be able to forgive himself.

Later that afternoon, Alex and Elise were lingering in the lobby, waiting for something, anything, to happen. They both heard Monique's door close upstairs, and as she walked down the steps, they both pretended to be busy.

"I'll see you later," Monique said as she reached the door. "And remember, my room is off limits while I'm a guest here."

"Got it," Alex said.

They waited until she was gone, and then Alex asked, "Should we take one more peek at her room? Jackson didn't even have a bag, so there's nothing to see there."

"I think we should stay out, for now," Elise said.

"Why, do you think she's coming back?"

"No," she admitted, "but it's not worth taking the risk."

"Let me just be sure that she's gone." Alex walked out onto the porch, looked around the parking lot, and saw that they were truly alone. When he got back in, Elise had poured two glasses of iced tea for them.

"Hope you don't mind, but I thought we could use a cool drink."

"Sounds great," he said as he killed half of it on the spot. He wasn't at all certain how she did it, but Elise's brew was as close to Evans Graile's tea as any he'd ever tasted.

As Alex sat on the couch, something poked him in the back. He'd forgotten all about the catalogue he'd taken from Monique's room, still stuffed in the back of his jeans. Flipping through it, he studied the marked items.

"What have you got there?" Elise asked.

"It was in Monique's trashcan. There's a pattern here that's interesting."

"What's that?"

"All of the items that are circled can be counterfeited," he said, showing her not just coins, but other monies and a painting as well.

"Do you think this was Tony's?"

Alex flipped through the pages until he found a small notation, written in pencil in a particular hand. It said, "Do the rewards outweigh the risks?"

"It's Tony's," Alex said. "I'd know his handwriting anywhere."

"What was Monique doing with it, then?"

"Beats me. After overhearing that conversation at the lighthouse base earlier, I can't imagine that she has any idea that the coins we found are fake."

"All but one," Elise corrected. "It's an important distinction. If she knows they're fake, all she's interested in is the one legitimate coin."

"And if she doesn't?"

"She agreed to the split, didn't she?" Elise asked.

"Not so fast, though. What if she agreed just to get her hands on the real one? If Jackson let her sort them, she could put the real one in her half. No, we can't count her out yet. She could be a dupe, but she could also be a coconspirator. Odds are, though, one of them did killed Tony."

"I think so, too" Elise said.

Alex chewed his lower lip. "Maybe we should turn this over to the sheriff right now. After all, we've narrowed it down quite a bit."

"Is that what you truly want to do?" Elise asked.

"What I want to do is find Tony's killer, so he can get some justice, and we can get married."

"Then I vote that we stick to the plan, at least for now," Elise said.

They both heard a car drive up. "I wonder if Jackson is back from his drive."

"Maybe Monique just came back to check on us. I have a hunch she doesn't trust us."

Alex grinned at that. "Imagine that."

Then, to their surprise, it was neither one of their suspects.

Mor and Emma were back, and what was more, they were each carrying a suitcase.

Chapter 9

What's with the luggage?" Alex asked as they opened the door.

"I was a little peckish, so I thought I'd pack a snack," Mor said with a big grin.

Emma slapped him playfully. "Can you give a straight answer to a question for once in your life, Mordecai?"

"Yes," he said solemnly without adding any inflection to it at all.

After a moment's pause, he added, "See? That was no fun at all."

Emma looked at Elise and asked, "Do boys ever become men?"

"I don't know, but I kind of like these two just the way they are."

Emma just shook her head. "Sometimes you are as bad as they are."

Alex said, "I'd love to stand around and chat about my shortcomings, but we have things to do. What's going on with the bags?"

"We're checking in," Mor said. "Emma here thought it might be better if we were on the scene, in case you needed us."

"You're checking in?" Elise asked.

"If it's okay with you."

"The more the merrier," Alex said.

Mor nodded. "Were you able to discover anything while we were gone?"

"Quite a bit, actually, but before we get into that, how did the coins turn out?"

"You tell me," Mor said as he reached into his jacket pocket and pulled out a felt bag. He handed it to Alex, who opened it and spilled the coins into his hand. From close up they most likely wouldn't fool anyone, but at first glance, they looked real enough. Not as good as Tony's counterfeits, but they couldn't use them. If this didn't work, Alex wanted to be able to present them to Sheriff Armstrong without having touched them since he and Mor had found the coins.

"These are nice," Alex said. "I can't even spot the real one."

"That's because it's here," Mor said, and held up the one true coin in their possession.

Once he saw it, the validity of the other coins was clearly debunked. "Don't worry," Mor said after seeing Alex's face. "They won't have this one to compare these with, and if we do this right, they won't have time to look too closely."

"Do you have any ideas?" Alex asked. He'd come up with, and discarded, several plans during the day, but he hadn't been completely satisfied with any of them.

"Not really." Mor took the coins from Alex and returned them to the pouch he'd brought them in.

"I hope you didn't make them in vain," Alex said.

"Are you kidding? I had a blast doing it." He handed the tied bag to Alex. "Besides, you'll come up with something."

"I'm glad you have faith in me," Alex said, "because I'm not sure I'll be able to think of anything at all."

"We all believe in you," Elise said, and Emma nodded as well.

"Then I don't have much choice, do I?" Alex's stomach rumbled. "Is anyone else hungry?"

"I could go for a bite," Mor said broadly.

Emma patted his stomach. "Why am I not surprised to hear you say that?"

"Hey, I have a high metabolism," Mor protested.

"It goes along nicely with your cholesterol level," she said.

Elise said, "I could make something here so we can keep an eye on things."

"I'll help," Emma said.

"What should we do in the meantime?" Alex asked.

"Figure out how to trap the killer," Elise said as she

kissed him lightly.

"Is that all?"

She patted him on the chest. "You can do it."

"Thanks. I just hope your faith isn't misplaced."

The last word triggered something in his mind, and Elise saw that he'd come up with something. "What is it?"

"I'm not sure yet. Mor, let's go over to the Main Keepers Quarters."

"I'm with you," he said.

"You two be careful," Emma said.

"What possible trouble could we get into?" Mor asked.

"Knowing the two of you, I don't even want to begin to speculate."

He laughed, kissed his wife, and the two of them started to leave the Dual Keepers' Quarters when they noticed two cars coming up the drive. Monique and Jackson were coming back, and they shouldn't see Alex and Mor.

It was starting to get dark out, and there was a chill in the air that promised the cooler temperatures that were sure to come. The leaves were starting to fade away and fall, but there were enough still on the trees to rattle as the wind blew through them.

As the two men hustled to the other building trying not to be seen, Mor said, "It's getting cold out."

"We're due, don't you think?"

As Alex unlocked the main door to the other building, Mor asked him, "What exactly did you have in mind?"

"I can't say until I see that room again," Alex said. He hoped Mor wouldn't ask him any more questions. He had a thought, more of a wisp of an idea, and if he gave it too much consideration, Alex knew that it could easily vanish.

His hand shook a little as he opened the door to the room where Tony had been murdered, but it was less now than it had been before. He wasn't exactly getting used to being there, but at least he could reenter the room without balking at the threshold.

Alex looked around the room, took it in, and then

nodded.

"I was right."

"About what?" Mor asked.

Alex held a hand up to silence his best friend as he tried to decide if he could use this new information as a way to trap the real killer.

Finally, he spoke. "I had it, but it's gone."

"Don't worry, it will come to you."

Alex shook his head. "But maybe not tonight. We need to find a way to keep either one of our suspects from sneaking in here tonight."

"I'll stay here," Mor said.

"I can't ask you to do that," Alex said. There was no way he could expect his friend to stay in a room where a murder had so recently occurred.

"You're not asking. I'm volunteering. We can spring our trap tomorrow night."

"What makes you think I'll be able to come up with something by then?"

"However long it takes," the big man said. "There's no time limit on my offer."

Alex couldn't bear the thought of Mor staying there. "Hang on. Let me think a minute."

Mor asked softly, "Would it help if I waited outside?"

"Do you mind?"

"I'll be on the other side of the door. Call me if you need me."

After he was gone, Alex looked around again. How could he trap the killer with the coins Mor had so carefully crafted? There had to be a way, if he could only see it.

And then it hit him. They were all being too clever. What mattered was that the murderer got the chance to come back to the scene of their crime. What if, as crazy as it sounded, the killer wasn't really after the coins, but something else? Say the piece of paper they'd found? Or even something else. There was only one way to find out. Alex took a towel from the bathroom, opened it, and tucked

Mor's coins inside, still housed safely in their bag. After putting the towel back in its place, he walked out to speak with Mor.

In a low voice, he said, "You need to go back to the inn and tell the ladies that I need to be alone. Tell them I'm going for a long drive and won't be back tonight. Make it convincing, and do it loudly enough so that Jackson and Monique can hear you. I know that you can bellow, so that shouldn't be a problem."

"What are you going to really be doing?"

He pointed across the hall at the linen closet. "I'll be hiding in there, watching to see what happens. Leave the main door unlocked when you go. We want to make it easy on our suspects, and we need them to come in that way,"

"I'll be back as soon as I can."

Alex put a hand on his friend's shoulder. "I'm sorry, but you can't. I'm counting on you to make up for my absence. Be loud, be funny, and most important, be noticed."

"Got it," Mor said.

Alex watched his best friend leave, and then he stepped into the closet. If he moved things around a little, he could see all the way down the hallway. If someone tried to get into the room where Tony had been killed, Alex would see it.

He passed the time remembering the times he and Tony had in the past. There weren't a lot of good memories, but he cherished the ones he had. Tony hadn't been much of a brother, but he'd stood up for Alex a few times, and Alex realized that he'd never thanked his brother for that, at least. And now it was too late.

Alex knew that Jackson was supposed to come while Monique distracted the others. At least that was the theory. Sure enough, Alex saw the hallway door open, and Jackson walked in as though he owned the inn. Going straight for the room where Tony had been killed, Alex waited for him to find the coins. The man was a real pro, and entered with a blade of some sort in his hand. Alex pulled back a little and watched him go into the room where Tony had been killed.

Ten minutes later, Jackson came out with the bag, the knife put away. Alex was about to jump out when he realized that didn't mean anything. Not only was he unarmed, but it still didn't prove that Jackson was a murderer. He could have met up with Tony there to discuss their business arrangement before the murder. Instead of leaving, Alex kept his vigil, and in less than five minutes, it was rewarded. The hallway door opened again, and this time Monique came through. Alex watched her, and to his surprise, he saw her going into the room next door, not the place where Tony was killed. What was she doing? And then he thought he knew.

Two minutes later she came out with a towel under her arm, and that's when Alex stepped out of the closet.

"I've been waiting for you," he said as he switched on a light. Enough had come through the windows before from the moon to give the space some illumination, but the fresh and direct light hurt his eyes. Alex was sorry that Jackson had gotten away. He would have liked to ask the man a few questions, but that was too bad.

"What are you doing here?" he asked Monique.

Before she had a chance to answer, Jackson came back, with Mor right on his heels.

"I thought you could use a little backup," Mor said.

"I didn't do anything wrong," Jackson said.

"He's got a knife," Alex said.

"I've got it," Mor said with a smile.

"Let me go," Jackson said, a look of hate in his eyes.

Mor put a hand on his shoulder and clamped down. As tough as Jackson was, Alex knew that it had to have hurt. "You're not going anywhere."

"Actually, she's the one you need to watch," Alex said as he pointed at Monique.

Chapter 10

"But he's the one who took the coins," Monique said in protest as Mor grabbed her as well. "I distracted you all so he could sneak in here and steal them. He was supposed to split them with me, but he was taking off. That's why I came over here to see what was going on."

Alex shook his head. "Don't you ever get tired of lying, Monique?"

"He killed Tony," she screamed. Mor's grip tightened on Monique's shoulder, and she stopped talking, at least for the moment.

"He might be a thief, but he didn't kill my brother," Alex said. "The coins weren't what were important here. You didn't care that Jackson took the coins. Well, maybe you cared, but it wasn't your top priority. Getting this was."

Alex reached down and picked up the tightly wrapped towel at his feet. As he opened it, the missing bathmat tumbled out onto the floor. "You got scratched during the argument with Tony, didn't you? Were you afraid your blood was on it, too?"

"I don't know what you're talking about," Monique said as she tried to cover one hand with another.

Alex continued. "I already saw your band-aid. Sure, we all thought the coins were the driving motive, but honestly, both of you had the opportunity and the motivation to steal from Tony. But only one of you had a reason to kill him." He turned to Jackson. "I'm not sure if the police can even arrest you with the evidence we've uncovered. After all, the fake coins Tony had and the ones we made up are all worthless."

Jackson looked surprised, and a little relieved, but then Mor added, "Don't forget about the real coin."

Jackson laughed, a cold and hard sound. "According to you people, I never had it. If had to guess, I'm willing to bet that it's in a safe somewhere around the inn, probably in your office."

It was clear to Alex that Jackson knew all about his safe, and what it held, including the piece of paper he and Mor had found, which Alex had brought along with him, just in case he needed it. The last thing Alex wanted was for Jackson and his boss to ever come back to the Hatteras West Inn. He took the paper from his pocket, and then handed it to Jackson.

"What do you get out of this?" Jackson asked suspiciously before he took the paper.

"I want you and your people to forget we ever existed."

Jackson seemed to take that in. "What about the money we lost, and the coin you still have?"

"Don't push your luck," Mor said.

Alex spoke up. "The coin was here, but it's on its way to the state museum in Raleigh. I donated it in my brother's name." It wasn't exactly true, but it soon would be. Alex didn't want any profit from the coin that had been a part of his brother's last con, and donating it in the Winston name was somehow fitting. "As for the rest of the fake coins, you can have them if you want them." He took the original bag of counterfeit coins from Elise and handed them to Jackson. "That should convince your boss that you were conned. As for the money, I don't have a clue what Tony did with it, but I can tell you this. It's not here."

"Good enough," Jackson said, and then started to walk away. Mor looked at Alex, and he shook his head. Alex was focused on one thing right now; the woman who had killed Tony.

"You're not going to just let him go, are you?" Monique cried out.

Alex didn't even have to answer. A squad car drove up the lane, its lights flashing and siren wailing. Jackson turned back and looked hard at Alex. "Did you set me up?"

"It wasn't us," Alex said.

Jackson shrugged, and then ate the piece of paper Alex

had just given him. "They don't have a thing on me." He tossed the coins back to Elise, and then wiped his hands on his pants. "We're good now."

As the sheriff got out of his car, Alex opened a window and called him over to them. Once he joined them in the Main Keeper's Quarters, Armstrong said, "There's a pileup on Old 70, but I got the call and came running. I was told there might be another murder here."

"Who called you?" Alex asked. He was amazed by how quickly the sheriff had shown up.

"It was anonymous," the sheriff admitted.

"Man or woman?" Alex asked.

"It was a woman."

"I made the call," Monique admitted. "I thought Jackson was going to kill me if I didn't turn the gold coins over to him."

"Why would I do that?" he asked. "I don't even know you, and we both know that the coins are counterfeit."

"Alex?" the sheriff asked. "You want to explain this to me?" He looked over at Mor. "I'm guessing you have a good reason to hold onto both of them."

"She killed my brother," Alex said.

"I suppose you have proof of that, right?"

"We do," Alex said.

"Then let's hear it."

Alex held the mat up. "If you send this to the crime lab, I'm willing to bet they'll find Tony's blood, and Monique's as well. They struggled during an argument, and she got scratched. Look at her hand if you don't believe me."

Monique said, "I caught it on a rusty nail somewhere around here. I should sue."

Alex shook his head, but the sheriff asked, "Is that all?"

"There are scuff marks in the room where Tony was killed. Whoever dumped him in the tub wasn't strong enough to pick him up, so they must have dragged him across the room. I noticed it the first time I was up there, but I didn't put it together with Tony's murder. If Jackson had killed him, he'd had no problem putting my brother over his shoulder and carrying him. The fact that Monique wasn't as strong made me suspect that she might have done it. Lastly, think about how Tony was killed. He was stabbed in the heart. What professional killer do you know that would use a knife to the heart? I've watched a lot of news and read quite a few mysteries my guests have left behind over the years. It sounds more like a crime of passion than of greed."

"Where'd the knife come from?" Armstrong asked, intently following Alex's words.

"I'd check her place if I were you," Alex said.

"Surely she's not that stupid," the sheriff answered.

"It's worth a shot, and it would tie it all up nicely if it turns out to be true, but I think you've got enough to arrest her."

"You meddling jerk," Monique said as she jerked away from Mor, reached into her jacket, and pulled out a gun. "I killed your brother, and now I'm going to get rid of all of you. What can they do, hang me more than once? I've already got Tony's blood on me. What's a little more going to hurt? I've got enough bullets to go around. Give me your gun, Sheriff," she said as she trained it on him.

Alex could see true madness in Monique's eyes. "Don't do it, Sheriff."

Armstrong looked at him as though he'd lost his mind. "Alex, I don't have any choice."

Alex knew that if Monique had the sheriff's gun, they would all be dead. He just had one option, and before he could talk himself out of it, he stepped forward towards Monique. Alex was willing to bet his life on the fact that Monique hadn't reloaded the gun. After all, he'd searched everywhere in her room and her purse. Where would she have gotten more ammunition?

Still, he felt his spine tingle as she turned the weapon on him and pulled the trigger as he rushed her.

Click.

Click.

Monique never got to pull it a third time.

Alex took it from her and handed it to the sheriff.

As Monique and Jackson were led away, Mor looked at his best friend and said, "I can't believe you pulled that off. You might have told me you took her bullets."

"There was no time," Alex explained. "Besides, I might have been wrong."

"You took one wail of a chance," Mor said.

"I had everything to lose if I let her have the sheriff's gun." He took Elise's hand in his, got down on one knee, and then said, "Elise, will you marry me?"

She threw herself onto him, knocking them both to the ground.

Alex laughed, and then asked, "Is that a yes?"

As she helped him up, Elise said, "I'm going to call my parents right now. As soon as they can get here, we're having that wedding."

Emma frowned. "There is no way we can pull this off without a week's notice, and that's pushing it."

Elise hugged Emma and said, "Don't get me wrong, I love what you did for our first wedding, but this one is going to be simple and clean. I just need my folks, you and Mor, and a preacher, and I'm fine."

"What about me?" Alex asked with a smile.

"You aren't getting out of my sight until we're married," Elise said. "I'm not about to take any more chances with us getting married."

"If you're waiting for me to protest, you're got a long wait."

"Then let's throw an impromptu wedding, shall we?" Elise asked.

She was answered by a chorus of yeses, and Alex was thrilled with the prospect of marrying Elise as soon as they could manage it.

The Last Chapter

The next afternoon offered them a beautiful day for their wedding.

Alex stood at the base of the lighthouse with Mor by his side. This wasn't the big affair that Alex and Elise had planned, but everyone who was important to them was there. Elise's parents had made it back to town, though just barely. Emma was with Elise in the inn, and the two men stood alone as the preacher was lost in his own thoughts.

"Nervous?" Mor asked Alex.

"I feel as though I've waited my entire life for this moment," Alex said. "I've found the love of my life, and I'm finally going to marry her."

Mor touched Alex's shoulder lightly. "Who would have believed in an hour that we'll both be married, two confirmed bachelors who used to take night cooking classes so they could meet women?"

"Are you happy?" Alex asked him.

He wasn't sure what kind of answer he was expecting, but most likely it would be housed in some type of joke. Mor surprised him, though.

"Alex, I know Emma and I might look like an odd match from the outside, but we're a perfect fit. The woman is crazy in all the right places, you know what I mean?"

"I get it," Alex said. "When I'm with Elise, it's like I've known her forever. Before she came to the inn, I never would have said that I believed in destiny, but I don't know how else to explain it."

"We're lucky men," Alex said.

"Gentlemen," Kyle said, "here they come."

Alex looked back toward the inn and saw Emma holding the door open for Elise. Emma started toward them, and then Elise came out, flanked by her father on one side and her mother on the other. He barely noticed them, though.

Elise was a beautiful woman, and Alex was very aware of it, but at that moment in time, she was nothing short of perfection. The white dress she wore flowed perfectly around her, and while he was no expert on these kinds of things, he could appreciate how wonderful she looked.

He thought he was seeing her at her most beautiful, but he was wrong.

When their gazes met, he saw her smile, warmly and broadly and full of love, and that's when he knew truly just how lovely she was.

Elise's parents walked with her, Emma leading the way, and as they approached the steps, Emma moved to be with Mor, while Elise's parents took the other side.

Elise put her hand on his, and Alex said softly, "Hey there."

"Hi yourself," she said as they turned to Kyle.

"Dearly beloved," the preacher began, but most of his words were lost on Alex.

And finally, the best question he'd ever been asked in his life was spoken aloud.

"Do you, Alex, take Elise, to be your lawfully wedded wife, to have and to hold, in sickness and in health, for richer and for poorer, from this day forward?"

"I do," he said.

"And do you, Elise, take Alex, to be your lawfully wedded husband, to have and to hold, in sickness and in health, for richer and for poorer, from this day forward?"

He hadn't realized he'd been holding his breath until he heard her say, "I do."

"Then by the authority of the state of North Carolina, I now pronounce you husband and wife," Kyle said. "You may kiss the bride."

Alex turned to her, took her in his arms, and before he kissed her, he said, "I love you."

"I love you, too," she answered, tears of joy tracking down her cheeks.

He kissed her then, and at that moment, Alex and Elise

Winston, husband and wife, started the rest of their lives together, with the lighthouse forever looking benignly over them.

Afterword

And that's it.

At least I think it is.

I've long wanted to write this book, and the one before it, Key to Murder. When I found out from my publisher that they wouldn't be renewing the Lighthouse Inn mystery series for books 6 and 7, I was more than a little taken aback. You see, in my mind, Alex and Elise always ended up together, married, and happily running the Hatteras West Inn long into their sunset years. It was an image I'd had from the very beginning, and I'd even written the first book with them ending up getting married on the spot. My editor didn't want that though, hoping for more of a Moonlighting feel, the old tv show where the viewers were constantly wondering whether the leads would get together or not in the end.

I most definitely wanted Alex and Elise together. It took a great amount of creativity to keep them apart over the first five books, and I wasn't the only one getting frustrated by the lack of their romantic progress. With just a little more time, I knew I could make my case to my editor.

But suddenly, the rug was pulled out from under me, and I was told that would be it. I asked if I could add a small section to the last book, Booked for Murder, and was told that it would be possible. It was a gracious move on Penguin's part allowing me to do it, one that I will be eternally grateful for.

Here is the section I added even as the manuscript was going off to be converted into a book.

Elise said, "Before we go in, there's something we need to talk about."

Alex asked, "Is it about us?"

"It is," Elise said solemnly. "I'm ready to answer your question."

Alex found himself holding his breath in anticipation as

he waited for his fate to be decided.

"Go ahead, I'm ready."

Elise said, "Alex, you've been the best friend I've ever had, and the thought of losing what we have right now is more than I can take."

He started to say something, but she held up one hand. "Please, just hear me out."

He nodded, not trusting himself to speak.

"I love Hatteras West almost as much as you do, and the thought of being forced to leave because something has broken between us is unbearable. And let's face it; my track record with relationships isn't all that sterling. I'm sorry, but I know this is true about me. All the signs point to us staying friends. There's just too much to risk losing."

Alex felt his heart explode in his chest, but he fought to keep from showing his devastation. He knew on one level that what she said was true, all of it; it still didn't make it any easier to accept.

Elise took a deep breath, then added, "That said, if you're willing to risk everything, then so am I."

It took him a second to realize that he'd just heard what she said. "Excuse me?"

She laughed slightly. "I said I'd love to pursue a relationship with you, starting right now."

Alex said, "Are you sure?"

"Oh, Alex, I think we've talked this to death. Let's just take a chance."

And then she kissed him.

It was the best I could do, given the state of things at the time.

I left the Lighthouse Inn behind, not by choice, and moved on to mystery series about candles, cards, soap, and several other things.

And then the playing field changed. I'd had the rights to my earlier books reverted to me as they went out of print, not sure what I was going to do with them, but happy to have them back in my hands. As ebook publishing began to take off, I saw that some folks were putting their backlists for sale, and I thought, why not? It would be nice to have copies available online, as I'd been asked time and time again for paperbacks that were now out of print. To my delight, the books began to sell. I started getting requests from readers, and they were so similar it was eerie.

They all wanted to know the same thing. "What happens next with Alex and Elise?"

I'd been wondering that myself, actually. I'd alluded to a lighthouse swap with another couple in Booked for Murder, and had planned to make that the sixth book, but the end of the contract meant the end of the series.

Then again, maybe not.

I got out my old copies and found myself being drawn back into the Lighthouse Inn mysteries myself. Alex's voice came back easily and unbidden to mind, and I could see the glorious structure of the lighthouse, the polished hardwood floors in the Dual Keepers' Quarters, and the formations of Bear Rocks as I considered the question, what happens next.

It was time to see what my old friends were up to.

My writing schedule was pretty brutal, but I carved out some time, and I wrote Key to Murder instead of taking a vacation.

SPOILER ALERT: IF YOU'RE THE TYPE THAT READS THE LAST BIT FIRST, YOU MIGHT WANT TO SKIP THIS SECTION IF YOU HAVEN'T READ KEY TO MURDER. GO ON, READ IT NOW. DON'T WORRY, WE'RE ALL VERY PATIENT HERE. WE'LL WAIT.

In Key to Murder, Alex and Elise finally make the lighthouse swap (not forever, but long enough to know there's no place like home), and much more importantly, along with solving another crime together, Alex admits his love for Elise, and when he thinks he's dying, he proposes. She accepts, and he fades away.

But not for good, obviously. I love their interaction at the hospital after Alex wakes up. Elise isn't sure how he'll feel, but Alex couldn't be more delighted. It took someone pulling a trigger to finally make Alex pull the trigger himself and propose. How appropriate is that?

END OF SPOILERS

And that leads us to this book, Ring for Murder. I've had that title floating around in my head for ten years, and I can't tell you what a joy it is to finally be able to use it.

I've said this is the finale of the Lighthouse Inn mysteries. After all, the story arc is completed. We see Alex and Elise meet for the first time in Innkeeping with Murder, endure untold hardships together, fall in love, and finally, get married on the steps of the lighthouse, the way I'd seen them ending up from the start.

But that doesn't necessarily mean that the series is finished forever. If I get an idea that I can't resist for another Lighthouse Inn mystery, whether it occurs before the wedding or after it, I'll probably write it as well. I can't say no to Alex and Elise, who gave me my first break in the publishing world and fulfilled a dream I'd harbored for several years, to see a novel of mine in print with my name emblazoned across it.

So don't hold me to it when I say this is the end.

But if it is, I can rest peacefully knowing that all is right with the world.

Alex and Elise are together, forever.

And the lighthouse continues to watch over them until the end of time.

Tim Myers
February 2011

Made in the USA
Lexington, KY
20 November 2013